Bola

He beg...
Ironma.. stood stock-still, the living embodiment of his own nickname as Bolan disassembled the bomb. The Executioner gripped the loose increment and slowly pulled it out.

"What's wrong?" Cervantes stared at the bomb. "Is it going to go off?" she asked.

Bolan examined the red LED display on the side. It was a timer and it read 00.00. "It already has," he said.

Cervantes recoiled. "If it's a nerve gas—"

Bolan shook his head. "It's not nerve gas. It's a biological agent. And we've been exposed."

He thumbed his throat mike to the Stony Man Farm frequency.

"Control, we have penetrated target. Threat is believed to be biological. Nature of agent is unknown. Biological agent is not contained. Repeat, biological agent is not contained."

MACK BOLAN®
The Executioner

- #260 Dayhunt
- #261 Dawnkill
- #262 Trigger Point
- #263 Skysniper
- #264 Iron Fist
- #265 Freedom Force
- #266 Ultimate Price
- #267 Invisible Invader
- #268 Shattered Trust
- #269 Shifting Shadows
- #270 Judgment Day
- #271 Cyberhunt
- #272 Stealth Striker
- #273 UForce
- #274 Rogue Target
- #275 Crossed Borders
- #276 Leviathan
- #277 Dirty Mission
- #278 Triple Reverse
- #279 Fire Wind
- #280 Fear Rally
- #281 Blood Stone
- #282 Jungle Conflict
- #283 Ring of Retaliation
- #284 Devil's Army
- #285 Final Strike
- #286 Armageddon Exit
- #287 Rogue Warrior
- #288 Arctic Blast
- #289 Vendetta Force
- #290 Pursued
- #291 Blood Trade
- #292 Savage Game
- #293 Death Merchants
- #294 Scorpion Rising
- #295 Hostile Alliance
- #296 Nuclear Game
- #297 Deadly Pursuit
- #298 Final Play
- #299 Dangerous Encounter
- #300 Warrior's Requiem
- #301 Blast Radius
- #302 Shadow Search
- #303 Sea of Terror
- #304 Soviet Specter
- #305 Point Position
- #306 Mercy Mission
- #307 Hard Pursuit
- #308 Into the Fire
- #309 Flames of Fury
- #310 Killing Heat
- #311 Night of the Knives
- #312 Death Gamble
- #313 Lockdown
- #314 Lethal Payload
- #315 Agent of Peril
- #316 Poison Justice
- #317 Hour of Judgment
- #318 Code of Resistance
- #319 Entry Point
- #320 Exit Code
- #321 Suicide Highway
- #322 Time Bomb
- #323 Soft Target
- #324 Terminal Zone
- #325 Edge of Hell
- #326 Blood Tide
- #327 Serpent's Lair
- #328 Triangle of Terror
- #329 Hostile Crossing
- #330 Dual Action
- #331 Assault Force
- #332 Slaughter House
- #333 Aftershock
- #334 Jungle Justice
- #335 Blood Vector

The Executioner — Don Pendleton's

BLOOD VECTOR

A GOLD EAGLE BOOK FROM
WORLDWIDE

TORONTO • NEW YORK • LONDON
AMSTERDAM • PARIS • SYDNEY • HAMBURG
STOCKHOLM • ATHENS • TOKYO • MILAN
MADRID • WARSAW • BUDAPEST • AUCKLAND

If you purchased this book without a cover you should be aware that this book is stolen property. It was reported as "unsold and destroyed" to the publisher, and neither the author nor the publisher has received any payment for this "stripped book."

First edition October 2006

ISBN-13: 978-0-373-64335-6
ISBN-10:   0-373-64335-7

Special thanks and acknowledgment to
Chuck Rogers for his contribution to this work.

BLOOD VECTOR

Copyright © 2006 by Worldwide Library.

All rights reserved. Except for use in any review, the reproduction or utilization of this work in whole or in part in any form by any electronic, mechanical or other means, now known or hereafter invented, including xerography, photocopying and recording, or in any information storage or retrieval system, is forbidden without the written permission of the publisher, Worldwide Library, 225 Duncan Mill Road, Don Mills, Ontario, Canada M3B 3K9.

All characters in this book have no existence outside the imagination of the author and have no relation whatsoever to anyone bearing the same name or names. They are not even distantly inspired by any individual known or unknown to the author, and all incidents are pure invention.

® and TM are trademarks of the publisher. Trademarks indicated with ® are registered in the United States Patent and Trademark Office, the Canadian Trade Marks Office and in other countries.

Printed in U.S.A.

In audacity and obstinacy will be found safety.
—Napoleon I, 1769–1821
Maxims of War

I believe in making a bold statement. No matter what the enemy resorts to, I will find a way to fight back.

—Mack Bolan

THE MACK BOLAN
LEGEND

Nothing less than a war could have fashioned the destiny of the man called Mack Bolan. Bolan earned the Executioner title in the jungle hell of Vietnam.

But this soldier also wore another name—Sergeant Mercy. He was so tagged because of the compassion he showed to wounded comrades-in-arms and Vietnamese civilians.

Mack Bolan's second tour of duty ended prematurely when he was given emergency leave to return home and bury his family, victims of the Mob. Then he declared a one-man war against the Mafia.

He confronted the Families head-on from coast to coast, and soon a hope of victory began to appear. But Bolan had broken society's every rule. That same society started gunning for this elusive warrior—to no avail.

So Bolan was offered amnesty to work within the system against terrorism. This time, as an employee of Uncle Sam, Bolan became Colonel John Phoenix. With a command center at Stony Man Farm in Virginia, he and his new allies—Able Team and Phoenix Force—waged relentless war on a new adversary: the KGB.

But when his one true love, April Rose, died at the hands of the Soviet terror machine, Bolan severed all ties with Establishment authority.

Now, after a lengthy lone-wolf struggle and much soul-searching, the Executioner has agreed to enter an "arm's-length" alliance with his government once more, reserving the right to pursue personal missions in his Everlasting War.

Washington, D.C.

They were in the house. It was four o'clock in the morning, and Mack Bolan was betting District of Columbia Federal Judge Shoshanah MacNight was not expecting company. He was also betting that the four young men who had crept out of the stolen minivan weren't collecting for the Red Cross.

Bolan came out of the trees.

The intruders had overcome the gate security and driven up the private drive with their lights off. Four had just broken into the house, and the getaway driver peered down the drive with a pair of night-vision goggles.

Bolan was wearing night-vision equipment as well. The crepe soles of Bolan's boots were silent as he walked up behind the van to the driver's door. The driver held a cell phone in one hand, ready to punch the emergency preset button in case of trouble. An Uzi submachine gun lay on the dashboard, and a cigarette burned in the driver's hand. It was clear he was not expecting trouble.

Bolan cleared his throat.

The goggled head whipped around, only to meet Bolan's fist. Lenses crunched beneath the Executioner's knuckles, and the driver's head rubbernecked. Teeth flew as the second blow unhinged the driver's jaw and draped him unconscious over the steering wheel. Bolan peered into the van, but there was no one else in the vehicle.

Suddenly a dog's snarl cut short into an agonized yip. Bolan's recon and securing of the vehicle had taken only heartbeats, but those were heartbeats too long. He snatched the van keys and ran through the open front door of the house. On the stairwell lay the bleeding body of a Border collie. The dog had been killed in midlunge by a blow from a machete.

Bolan moved up the stairs, noting the bloodstains on the risers as he drew two .45 caliber United States Special Operations Command pistols. He pushed up his night-vision goggles as a light flicked on at the top of the stairs. Judge MacNight screamed from the bedroom and a guttural snarl answered, "Shut up, bitch!" The sound of flesh hitting flesh cut off the judge's second scream.

Bolan entered the bedroom with his guns leveled.

Four Latino males surrounded the judge at the foot

of the queen-sized sleigh bed. All four had stripped off their T-shirts and their bodies and faces crawled with gang tattoos. The judge's black silk pajama top was half torn away. They had forced her to her hands and knees, and a hugely muscled man held the woman's forearms across the curling wooden edge of the bed. A skinny man with a goatee yanked the judge's head back cruelly by her short, dark hair and clamped a tattooed hand over her mouth. The third man had a shaved head covered with the tattoo of a spiderweb, and he stood slightly off to the side holding a sawed-off shotgun. The fourth held a machete poised over Shoshanah Mac-Night's wrists. He spoke English with a thick Spanish accent.

"You shoulda kept your hands out of our business! Now look what's happening to you! Huh? Now look what happens to you!" He took the machete in both hands like a samurai warrior. "You see what's gonna happen? You ain't ever puttin' your hands in anyone's business again! You ain't gonna have no hands!"

The judge shrieked beneath the hand smothering her mouth. Her eyes flew wide with horror as the man rested the machete against her wrists for a moment and then raised the blade over his head. She thrashed against the men holding her, but the man held her arms pinned at the foot of the bed like a vise.

The man with the machete smiled. "Will counsel please approach the stumps?"

The other three men laughed uproariously at the joke. It seemed they'd all seen the inside of a courtroom before.

Bolan cleared his throat again.

The weapons were the priority. Both of Bolan's pistols had accessory rails beneath the slides, and both of his pistols were highly accessorized. He extended his left hand and triggered the pepper-spray module. A high-pressure stream of mist spewed forth in a fan. The gunman screamed, dropping his shotgun and clawing at his eyes as the cloud of bear-strength pepper spray engulfed his head.

Bolan thrust out his right-hand pistol, and the stungun module beneath the barrel chuffed. A pair of barbs flew out trailing wires and sank into the machete man's naked chest. The soldier pressed the switch and the stun gun fired. The man let out a growl as his teeth clenched and his elbows pulled in against his sides. His machete slid out of his spasming hands as he fell to the floor.

The big man released the judge's hands and scooped up the fallen blade. The teardrop tattoos trailing down both cheeks and his professional wrestler's physique were clear indications that he had spent years pushing the heavy iron in a U.S. maximum security penitentiary and had killed men inside. The muscleman lunged toward the muzzles of Bolan's guns, machete poised for slaughter.

"Gonna kill you, man!" he screamed.

Bolan hit him in the face with a blast of the pepper spray. The bear spray was rated against Alaskan grizzlies, double the strength police were allowed to use against human suspects. It had been designed to deter beasts rather than men, but the man charging Bolan had spent years in the animal factory. Hard time forged his body and his mind-set for murder. He had undoubtedly been doused with pepper spray many times during his incarceration, and he was clearly ready to die.

The spray threw off his machete swing.

Bolan sidestepped the wild, whistling cut and blurred into a series of blows designed to break the big man down. He chopped the slide of his three-and-a-half-pound pistol into the man's wrist, and the machete fell as bone fractured. Bolan's backhand blow flayed open the guy's tattooed face and cracked the cheekbone. The Executioner drove his heel into the side of the big man's knee, and the joint popped and collapsed inward as the iliotibial band snapped. The giant tottered and Bolan swung his pistol like an ax, slamming the slide into the side of the bull-like neck to crush the carotid artery and nerve bundle.

The big man fell to the floor.

The fourth man knelt on the bed in shock. The battle had lasted a few scant seconds. He suddenly snapped out of his stupor and snaked his forearm under MacNight's chin. Spittle flew from his lips in a scream. "I'll kill her!"

"Really?" Bolan cocked his head as he stepped forward. "How?"

"I'll..." The skinny gangster tensed in fear and rage. "I'll snap her neck! I'll wring her neck like a fuckin' chicken!"

The judge gasped as the arm tightened around her throat.

Bolan raised a questioning eyebrow. He knew breaking a human neck was difficult. He could do it about half a dozen different ways. The big man unconscious on the floor could have done it with brute force. Bolan had his doubts about the man holding the judge, but he had no doubt about the gangster's intentions.

"I'll kill the bitch! I'm telling you, man! One more step and I'll kill her!"

Bolan raised both .45s. The two pistols clicked as he pushed off the safeties. "I'll kill *you*," he said.

The judge stared at the Executioner like a deer caught in headlights.

"I..." The gangster's eyes scanned the room wildly as Bolan continued to step forward. The would-be killer came to some kind of decision. He reared up, holding the judge in front of him and squeezed his face against hers defensively. His free hand reached for something behind his back.

Bolan lunged and threw a right-hand lead—only his fist was filled with the blackened steel mass of the pistol. The muzzle punched directly between the gangbanger's eyebrows. The man collapsed instantly. A switchblade fell to the sheets unopened.

Judge MacNight knelt shaking on the bed. Her bedroom was a sea of broken, moaning men. She blinked and clutched her torn pajama top to her chest. Her left cheek was swelling where she'd been slapped, and her hair was in disarray. Despite that, the woman, in her early fifties, was an aristocratically beautiful woman. "Who..." She found her voice. "Who are you?"

The original machete man was recovering from being electrocuted and had pushed himself to his hands and knees.

"One moment, Your Honor," Bolan said.

Judge MacNight flinched as the soldier knelt and chopped the butt of his pistol into the base of the man's head. The thug resumed his prone position on the floor. Bolan rose and holstered his pistols. He took the judge's robe from the back of a chair and draped it across her shoulders.

"Thank you." She shivered as she pulled the robe around her, and she watched as Bolan went about hogtying the gangsters with elastic restraint strips. "Who are you, again?"

"I'm representing the Justice Department."

The judge considered this. "Do you know who these men are?"

"I believe they are members of Mara Salvatrucha 13."

Judge MacNight stared about at the carnage in confusion. "MS-13? I'm...not working on any case involving them."

Bolan nodded thoughtfully as he picked up the phone and dialed 911. "I know."

Stony Man Farm, Virginia

The blonde Fox cable news anchor read the morning headlines. "'In what appears to be a brutal case of mistaken identity, Judge Shoshanah MacNight was attacked in her home early this morning. The men perpetrating the attack are allegedly members of the El Salvadoran street gang Mara Salvatrucha, also known as MS-13. Viewers may recall that in the past month two District of Columbia judges have been similarly attacked. One was slain, and one was mutilated with a machete. Both were trying first-degree murder cases against alleged MS-13 gang members. Judge MacNight was unharmed, and five suspects were apprehended by private security. Judge MacNight has never tried a case involving MS-13 activities. In international news, Russian prime minister...'"

"Judge MacNight." Aaron "The Bear" Kurtzman clicked off the television and shook his head in amusement as he and Bolan sat in the kitchen and drank coffee. "I don't agree with all of her decisions, but that is one sharp lady. They say she's a shoo-in for a Supreme Court nomination." He sighed wistfully. "Good-looking, too. You know she modeled to put herself through law school?"

Bolan changed the subject diplomatically. "I asked you for an intelligence asset. Any luck?"

"As a matter of fact, yes." Kurtzman turned his gaze to the kitchen clock. "She should be here any time now."

"She?"

Both men looked up as the windowpanes began to shake with the unmistakable rhythm of rotors. They looked out the window as the Huey helicopter descended. The chopper's skids came down on the lawn, and the cabin door slid back. Two Farm blacksuits jumped out. They reached back and assisted their blindfolded passenger to the ground. She was short, wearing faded jeans, a well-tailored black leather suit jacket, with a low-cut white camisole beneath. The barely restrained flesh was a pleasing olive complexion, and a federal badge on a neck chain lay against it. Her shoulders were broad, her waist narrow and her hips flared out again in a curvy, hourglass shape. She removed her blindfold and blinked against the Virginia sun. Her glossy black hair was pulled back into a loose ponytail. She had big dark eyes, big cheekbones, big lips and a big chin. Her face was more sensuous than beautiful, and Bolan liked what he saw.

"Latin spitfire," Kurtzman muttered.

The blacksuits ushered the woman toward the main farmhouse. Kurtzman tapped on the kitchen window to announce his location.

As she walked, Bolan caught glimpses of the gleaming stainless-steel mass of a 10 mm Smith & Wesson FBI Model 1076 in a left-handed cross-draw holster beneath her jacket.

"Big gun on the little lady," Bolan said.

"I wouldn't call her 'little lady' to her face," Kurtzman replied, as the woman joined them.

The woman cocked a bemused, coal-black eyebrow as she took in the two men sitting in the breakfast nook.

"Special Agent Candelaria Cervantes," Kurtzman said, "allow me to introduce you to Mathew Cooper."

The FBI agent held out her hand. Her eyes said she highly suspected the name was an alias. "Pleased to meet you. Call me Candy. Everybody does."

"Call me Matt." Bolan shook her hand. "I'm told you're the FBI Gang Investigation Unit's number one authority on MS-13."

"That's me." Cervantes said, smiling. "I was in it from '89 to '92."

"Really," Bolan said.

"I'd show you my tattoos, but I don't know you that well, yet."

Kurtzman took out a file. "I assume you've heard about the attack on Judge MacNight?"

"Oh, I heard about it, all right. That's my beat. I've been spearheading the investigation on the attacks on the other two judges. I was at D.C. General two hours ago. Those are some very bad boys. Two of them are wanted for murder in Honduras, and the big one, Florio, just did a ten-year stretch in Leavenworth." She looked hard at Bolan and Kurtzman. "You know, to take down those guys, I would have sent an FBI Fast Reaction Team. I would have expected them to go down in a blaze of glory, and I wouldn't be surprised if we took casualties doing it. It's kind of hard to believe that all five of them were taken alive by some ex-cop private security guards without a shot being fired."

"They weren't," Bolan admitted. "I did it."

"I was at the hospital. I saw them. They'd been professionally pistol-whipped." Agent Cervantes stared incredulously. "You took out all five? Hand to hand?"

"I wanted them alive and answering questions."

The special agent ran her dark eyes up and down Bolan's frame, looking impressed. "You won't get much. MS-13 doesn't talk. They die if they do."

"Maybe we can convince them," Bolan said.

"I'd love to see that. But what I'd really like to know is why you staked out MacNight's house," Cervantes countered. "She wasn't on the list of judges the FBI was watching. She was off our radar completely."

Bolan nodded at Kurtzman. "He's the one who pointed me in the right direction."

"There have been two attacks against federal judges by Mara Salvatrucha 13 in the past month. That sent up red flags with me, because two years back I'd read a report that said al Qaeda representatives had met with MS-13 leaders in Honduras."

"I read that report, too," Cervantes said.

"Yes, but this month I got a hold of another report stating that intelligence assets believed that al Qaeda lieutenants had met with MS-13 representatives again in Mexico City."

"I didn't hear that." Cervantes's brows lowered slightly. "Where'd you get that? CIA?"

Kurtzman smiled sadly. The fact was that even after 9/11, in many ways the CIA and the FBI were still hostile, territorial, mutually antagonistic camps. "Yes." He shoved the file over. "That got me thinking. Judge Mac-Night is currently involved in a case against a D.C. mosque accused of aiding and abetting al Qaeda sleeper cells. Her gardening and housecleaning has normally been done by Mexican-American domestic services. When I did a little digging, I found out that this month her normal services had to drop out for numerous reasons and El Salvadorans had filled in."

Cervantes smiled. "Well, that's how we connected the dots with the other two judges. The same El Salvadoran landscaping service had done their yards and recommended their domestics to them."

"I know. That's when I got my hunch about Judge

MacNight." Kurtzman grinned. "That's how they got in. MS-13 strong-armed the landscapers and the domestics, and got them to make impressions of the keys to the house and give them the security layouts. MS-13 gangsters were probably pretending to be workers at the time."

"So, you had Cooper, here, stake out the judge's house on a hunch?"

Bolan gazed at Cervantes with utmost seriousness. "You pay attention to his hunches, you live longer."

Special Agent Cervantes peered back and forth between the two men. "And who are you guys again?"

Bolan changed the subject. "I need you to give me more of an idea of who these MS-13 guys are. They aren't operating like normal gangbangers."

"You know I've been told to offer you any and all assistance possible, but I'll tell you up front I really don't like this spooky shit. Much less being kept in the dark."

Bolan was silent.

Cervantes frowned slightly as she looked back into her memories. "MS-13 has changed a lot since I was a member. Mara Salvatrucha stands for La Mara, a street in San Salvador and the Salvatrucha guerrillas that fought in the Salvadoran civil war. More than a million Salvadorans fled to the U.S. My family was among them."

"Your father was in the war?" Bolan asked.

"No, my father was a pig farmer. He wasn't on anybody's side. But that didn't stop the army from drafting my two brothers at gunpoint, or the rebels from 'liberating' our farm. They burned it down, slaughtered all the livestock and took my sister for a *campesina,* or 'camp girl.' We fled. Most Salvadorans emigrated to L.A. or D.C. and settled in the Hispanic communities. My family and thousands of others settled in Los Angeles, but we weren't well accepted. Our customs and dialect were different. We were outsiders, fresh off the boat, and ready-made victims for the Mexican gangs.

"MS-13 actually started out as an almost benevolent association. Their initial purpose was to defend Salvadoran immigrants from other gangs. Many MS-13 members were former rebel soldiers, and they violently defended Salvadoran turf in the barrios."

Cervantes sighed. "Of course, like any street gang that's created to defend an ethnic group, their purpose quickly perverts into preying on their own community."

Bolan considered the information. "What's their mainline business?"

"That's one of the problems. Some gangs specialize in drugs, others theft. MS-13's motto is any crime, any time. South American drug cartels use them as conduits to get narcotics into the U.S. In San Salvador, a hand grenade sells for two dollars, an M-16 for two hundred, so gun running and illegal weapon sales is a huge business for them. Another is exporting stolen cars to South America. According to FBI estimates, up to eighty percent of the cars being driven in El Salvador were stolen in the United States. Plus they're into all the usual stuff such as prostitution, extortion, burglary. If they see the opportunity, they take it. If you're a criminal and they see you in business, they'll try to take it over or make you pay a 'tax' to operate without interference.

"MS members across the country have started coming together in the last five years to unite into affiliated groups, receiving leadership from California and as far away as El Salvador."

"They're no longer a bunch of street gangs," Bolan said. "They're a mafia."

Cervantes nodded. "In normal street gangs, you just get jumped in. They beat the crap out of you when you go in and again if you ever leave. Blood in, blood out. In MS, you have to commit a violent act to prove your commitment and get your letters or symbols tattooed. According to informants, if you want to reach the higher echelons, you have to kill or at least assault a cop."

Kurtzman shook his head in disgust. "Nice."

"They routinely assault or kill judges, cops and local politicians in El Salvador. Beheading is their favorite calling card. Chopping off people's hands as a lesson or warning is another."

"Tell me more about their U.S. operations," Bolan said.

"The bad news is they're spreading. They've moved out from L.A. and D.C. into Oregon, Alaska, Texas,

Nevada, Utah, Oklahoma, Illinois, Michigan, New York, Maryland, Virginia, Georgia, Florida, and Canada and Mexico. They own chunks of Honduras and are intimately tied to crime on the U.S./Mexico border. Some reports indicate they control entire sections of it."

"There can't be that many Salvadoran immigrants," Kurtzman said.

"You'd be surprised. Nearly twenty percent of all Salvadorans live abroad, and ninety percent of those are in the United States." Cervantes shook her head. "But you're right. Originally, only Salvadorans were allowed membership. But recently, MS-13 has begun recruiting Ecuadorians, Guatemalans, Hondurans and Mexicans. They recently broke the Latino race barrier and have even recruited some African Americans, but most members are still recruited based on the basis of Central American ethnicity, and they exclusively form the top ranks of the leadership."

Cervantes leaned back wearily. "In short, you're right, Matt. They've got the organization of a mafia but with the violent mentality of a street gang. Their members tend to be utterly loyal and unafraid of the police or incarceration. They are very difficult to infiltrate and absolutely willing to kill."

It was a worst-case law-enforcement scenario, except that Bolan wasn't a cop. He was a soldier, and he thought like one. "Who are their enemies?"

Cervantes smiled at the question, seeing where

Bolan's mind was moving. "Well, just about every other gang in the U.S. is their enemy. Particularly the Latino gangs in Northern California. But if MS-13 is afraid of anything, it's La Sombra Negra."

Kurtzman's brow furrowed. "The Black Shadow?"

Bolan nodded. "The El Salvadoran death squads."

"Aren't they supposed to be out of business?" Kurtzman asked.

Cervantes shook her head. "That's what most of the world would like to believe and what a lot of Salvadorans like to tell themselves."

Bolan considered all he'd heard. "What do these guys want?"

"Anything they can get their hands on." Cervantes frowned quizzically. "What do you mean?"

"I want to do a hard probe, and I need bait. What's going to get the MS-13 boys all hot and bothered?"

Cervantes chewed her lip in thought. "Handguns."

Bolan nodded. "Oh yeah?"

"They have access to military materials, but street intelligence indicates that they often have difficulty obtaining handguns. Pistols just aren't readily available in El Salvador. They have no small-arms industry, and neither do any of her neighbors. Only military officers and police are issued pistols, so there are few in the country to steal. For most gang activity, a pistol is the weapon of choice and in the capital, they go at a premium. In fact, demand is so high that MS-13 cliques in the U.S. will sometimes take handguns as payment for drug transactions."

Bolan saw a plan coming together. "Bear, I need some pistols, a lot of them. Something sexy and plausible. Get Cowboy on it. Then I need to talk to Gadgets. Meantime, Judge MacNight was working on an al Qaeda sleeper cell case. I need you to find me an MS-13 connection here in D.C. Start with the boys in the hospital. They're probably cutouts, but we might get lucky. And get me everything there is on that cell."

"You got it. A pleasure to meet you, Agent Cervantes," Kurtzman said as he wheeled himself out of the kitchen, his mind already turning to the problem.

Bolan turned back Cervantes and flashed his most winning smile. "You in?"

The FBI agent blinked. "In?"

"I'm going to roll against MS-13, and I could use someone who speaks the lingo and knows the culture. I can extend your duty into a field assignment, if you're interested."

Candy Cervantes leaned forward and turned her smile to full wattage. "This I gotta see."

Charlottesville, Virginia

"Target in sight, Striker."

Mack Bolan brought up his night-vision goggles and looked through the windshield. A truck drove with its lights off toward the construction site. "Roger that, Candyman, target in sight."

Bolan clicked off his cell phone and slid out of the gleaming black civilian Hummer. Carl "Ironman" Lyons jumped down from the passenger side.

They looked dangerous, but not like two of the most dangerous operators on Earth.

Candelaria Cervantes was stationed a hundred yards back on the balcony of an unfinished town house behind a Remington M-700 Light Tactical sniper rifle. The meet was set at the site of a gated community that was under construction outside the Charlottesville suburbs.

A battered old Ford F-150 creaked and rumbled between the half-finished structures and whined to a halt.

The headlights flicked on, and Bolan and Lyons were spotlighted in the glare. Two men got out of the truck cab, while a third stayed behind the wheel. Two more jumped out of the bed, while one stayed crouched behind the cab holding an M-16 rifle.

Bolan measured the men as they approached. Many MS-13 members sported huge tattoos on their faces, proclaiming their affiliation. The four men before him were dressed in filthy jeans and T-shirts and equally beat-up baseball caps. Work gloves had been thrust into their pockets, and their faces were streaked with sweat and dust. Rakes, brooms and pole-pruners stood up from the back of the truck. The handles of a pair of lawnmowers hung out over the gate. Bolan remembered Cervantes's words. MS-13 was often brazen in its gang activity, but its members were equally adept at being chameleons. The four men who stepped forward looked like nothing more than dirty and weary day laborers getting off after a very long day of work.

Lyons held a folding stock Mini-14 rifle loosely, and Bolan rested a hand on the butt of the .44 Magnum Desert Eagle thrust under his belt.

A short, thin man grunted in thickly accented English. "Don't know you."

"I'm Odin." Bolan jerked his head at Lyons. "That's Thor. We don't know you either, amigo."

The leader spoke to a fat guy on his left without taking his eyes off Bolan. "Check 'em for wires."

Bolan slowly drew his Desert Eagle and spread his leather jacket by the corners. He allowed a very professional pat down, then smoothed his clothing. Lyons raised his rifle overhead and endured the same. Bolan smiled, the Desert Eagle dangling in his hand. "And you, amigo."

Bolan was impressed by the gang's professionalism. They didn't waste time with pat downs. One at a time, each man simply pulled up his T-shirt, dropped his pants and did a slow turn.

Bolan nodded. "So we're cool?"

The thin man stared unblinkingly at Bolan for long seconds. The rest of his crew watched Lyons, cocking their heads, glaring and posturing, sniffing for signs of weakness in the strangers. Lyons affected a crazed stare and smiled back.

The leader stared at Bolan like a stone Buddha. He slowly raised his hands together, forming the *M* gang sign with his fingers before jamming his thumbs into his chest. "Tuco." His hands fell back to his sides. "What'cha got, man?"

Bolan dropped the back gate of the Hummer and pulled out a large, plastic trunk. He flipped the latches open and gestured at the treasure within. Ten pistols lay nestled in custom-cut foam packing. "I got Glocks," he said.

"Glocks are good." The gangster pulled up his shirt again, showing his 9 mm Glock 17. "I got a Glock. Lemme see 'em."

"These are better than good." Bolan pulled out a pistol. "These Glocks? These are special."

Tuco hawked and spit, unimpressed.

Bolan sighed. "Allow me to demonstrate."

Tuco shrugged noncommittally.

Bolan racked the slide on the Glock 18C select-fire pistol. All the gangsters tensed except Tuco, who acted like the world could end for all he cared. Out of the corner of his eye Bolan caught the rifleman in the truck bed drawing a bead on him. The soldier pointed the gun at a berm of dirt where he'd propped a panel of drywall. He had drawn a human silhouette with a smiley face for a head on the panel. Saucer-sized circles formed targets over the groin, belly, heart and the head.

Bolan pressed the ambidextrous switch, and the internal laser sight mounted in the recoil guide tube beneath the barrel blinked into life. A ruby red dot appeared on the silhouette's crotch. "Amigo, where the dot goes, the bullets go."

Bolan flicked the selector lever to full-auto and squeezed the trigger. The gangsters flinched as the machine pistol snarled a 5-round burst into the silhouette's groin. He instantly whipped the ruby red dot up through the belly and heart circles, leaving ragged craters in the drywall like precision meteor strikes. The last four rounds obliterated the smiley face above the eyebrows.

Bolan lowered the empty pistol as the last of the flying shell casings hit the dirt. "You just point, pull, and pow-pow-pow." The Executioner smiled like Satan himself. "I told you, amigo—special."

"That's government shit," Tuco said, clearly suspicious. "Where'd you get it?"

Bolan shook his head. "The American government doesn't use machine pistols. These were made in Austria and modified here in the States. Their final destination was Argentina, for VIP protection."

"So how'd you get 'em?" Tuco asked.

Bolan spoke truthfully. "Some people I know had them intercepted. *How* is my business."

Bolan and Tuco exchanged stares. Bolan checked his watch. "You know, I could be getting laid," he said.

Tuco spoke grudgingly. "I'll take all ten."

"Ten?" Bolan thumped the crate. "That's just the top layer. I got fifty."

"You have...fifty?" Tuco finally registered some emotion.

"Fifty, with a spare magazine for each. They're all loaded, but more ammo is your problem. But there's a catch."

Tuco scowled. "What the fuck are you talking about?"

Bolan held out the pistol to Tuco. "You see that?"

Tuco took the hot gun in his hand. "Yeah?"

"Like I said, that ain't U.S. government shit. So, you start lighting up people in D.C., there will be an investigation. They'll be looking under every rock, and sooner or later that shit could come back to haunt me. Now, on the other hand, people start getting greased in San Salvador?" Bolan smiled slyly. "Dude, no harm, no foul. No one around here will give a crap. It was headed south anyway. Who knows who stole it. Know what I'm saying?"

Tuco didn't answer. He turned to the fat guy to his left. They began a rapid conversation. The Spanish was so fast and so full of Salvadoran slang Bolan could hardly understand it. The fat man turned and pulled a Blackberry out of his pocket. He began text-messaging someone. After about five minutes, he finally turned to Tuco and nodded.

Tuco smiled for the first time. It was the smile of a shark. "We'll take all fifty."

Stony Man Farm, Virginia

"WHAT HAVE YOU GOT, Bear?" Bolan, Lyons and Cervantes entered Aaron Kurtzman's domain. Kurtzman sat before a six-foot, high-definition flat screen staring at a glowing map of Virginia. Computer desks and monitors were arrayed around the room with the big screen dominating the far wall. On the map, a tiny blob of dots was moving slowly.

"I've got fifty signals moving north." Kurtzman spun his wheelchair to face his guests. "That was a gorgeous plan, Striker."

It had been a gorgeous plan. Between the firearms expertise of John "Cowboy" Kissinger and the mechanical wizardry of Herman "Gadgets" Schwarz, it had all come together. Kissinger had found the path and Schwarz had walked it.

Schwarz had taken apart the laser assemblies of the pistols and added a simple radio transmitter to each one. He had replaced the standard batteries with very powerful custom lithium models, but the power drain would still kill the power cells within a week and half. But that would be enough. He had chosen an odd end of the spectrum frequency, and each of the pistols pulsed on that frequency with a slightly different signature sequence.

A low altitude National Security Agency observation satellite had been tasked with monitoring the frequency, and its high-resolution thermal-imaging eye watched unblinkingly as the weapons moved up Highway 15 toward Washington. Two U.S. military observation satellites were adjusting their orbits, one to peer at Los Angeles and the California-Mexico border and the other at El Salvador.

A Glock machine pistol was a high-ticket item. A few would probably be retained by the local MS-13, but Bolan suspected most would be shipped as tribute to the Mara Salvatrucha leaders and their cronies in Los Angeles and San Salvador.

Candy Cervantes glanced around the room. "Bond, very Bond."

"So what's your next move?" Kurtzman asked.

"I'm going to give those Glocks a little time to migrate. Meantime, I think I'd like to set another trap for the MS-13 boys," Bolan said.

Kurtzman knew from long-suffering experience exactly where Bolan was going. "You're going to stick your head out and see who comes to chop it off."

"Or at least my hands," Bolan agreed. "MS-13 is big into vengeance, and right now they have five guys in the hospital. Candy, I want your informants to tip off MS-13 to the whereabouts of the security guy who took down their hitters at the judge's house."

"You're just going to let them take a shot at you?" Cervantes asked.

"Yeah, but they're smart, so you're going to have to make something up that they can verify. Like I got suspended for being too brutal and violating civil rights or something, and my private security license has been revoked pending review. License and gun taken, the whole bit. I want them to think I'm a former badass who's lost his power in this world and is a prime target for payback."

Bolan turned to Kurtzman. "Find me a rat hole in a bad part of D.C. Give these guys a good killing ground, someplace they'll feel secure about going to, making a hit and getting out of."

Kurtzman had run the scenario so many times he didn't bother to object. "I'm on it."

Bolan turned to Lyons. "I'm going to be armed for the Apocalypse, but I want you to be my ace in the hole."

Lyons rolled his eyes. He already considered himself in for the duration. "I got nothing better to do."

Bolan spun his chair to face Cervantes. "You down with this?"

Cervantes took a seat. "I'm in."

"She's on her way up, Striker." Barbara Price's voice came across the satellite link from Stony Man Farm.

The Executioner lay on the bed in a third floor room of the Patriot's Rest. It had once been a decent little hotel, but time and tide had left it in a very bad part of downtown Washington. "Roger that, Control. We have any friends?"

"I have a very suspicious van parked across the street and another one out back."

"What's suspicious about them?" Bolan asked.

"Satellite recon indicates one of your Glocks is in the van out back."

Bolan glanced at Lyons. "Candy's coming up, we have vans front and back. The one in front is confirmed hostile."

Lyons racked the bolt on his Remington semi-automatic 11-87 "entry" shotgun in answer.

Someone knocked on the door three times. "Hey, baby! Open up!"

Bolan waited a few seconds, and Agent Cervantes shrieked and pounded on the door again. "Hey! Asshole! You want your date or what!"

Bolan rose and went to the door. He peered out the peephole. Special Agent Cervantes was dressed in a pair of hot pink Lycra shorts and bikini top. She tottered in front of the door in white stiletto heels, and her fist crashed angrily into the door as gutter Spanish streamed from her mouth. "Don't waste my time! I got a big black pimp who's gonna kill your white—"

Bolan unchained the door and threw it open. Cervantes took a step back as Bolan loomed unshaved, clad in boxer shorts and a stained T-shirt. She flinched under Bolan's hostile glare. "Hey, baby. I'm Candy. You're a big one."

"Shut up, bitch," Bolan growled. "Get in." He noted two cleaning ladies down the hall as he grabbed the undercover agent's arm roughly, drew her into the room and slammed the door shut. The Patriot's Rest wasn't the kind of place that had a cleaning service. He slapped his right hand into his left like a thunderclap three times and Cervantes shrieked on cue as if she was being beaten.

He put his headset back on. "What's the deal on the cleaning ladies?" he asked.

Cervantes's red-painted lips parted in a predatory grin. "They were talking Salvadoran when I came up, and one was talking into a cell phone. You've been cased forward and back."

"They know Carl's in here?"

"No, I spent a few seconds in the stairwell listening. They said you were in your room watching TV by yourself and that you'd been drinking all day."

Lyons shot Bolan a rare smile. He'd entered the Patriot earlier in the day in a brown coverall and checked the air-conditioning in all the rooms. After a thorough recon, he'd scaled the side of the hotel to Bolan's fire escape and slid inside.

Bolan nodded to himself. The trap was set. Mara Salvatrucha thought he'd spent the day in a seedy hotel by himself, drunk, unarmed, and now he was spending the night with a hooker. It was a best case, pants-down, surprise assassination scenario for the bad guys.

Only the tables were about to be turned.

Bolan thumbed his throat mike. "Control, Candyman's in place. What's our status?"

Barbara Price spoke over the satellite link. "You have four coming in from the front. Someone just opened the back door and let in three more."

"Copy that, Control," Bolan replied.

Cervantes went to the tool bag Lyons had brought with him and withdrew a Heckler & Koch MP-5 submachine gun. She pulled out the telescoping stock and checked the loads in the weapon. Bolan and Cervantes both shrugged into body armor.

"We've got seven hostiles, on their way up. Possible hostiles already inside," Bolan said.

Cervantes's eyes widened as Bolan drew a pair of Beretta 93-R machine pistols, checked the loads and pushed the selectors of both pistols to 3-round-burst mode.

Bolan hooked his Pittsburgh Pirates baseball cap with the compensated muzzle of one of his Berettas. He went to the door and plastered himself against the wall to one side of it as Lyons and Cervantes crouched in opposite corners of the room and put the door in a cross fire.

They only had moments to wait before someone pounded and demanded entry. "Open up!"

Bolan nodded at Lyons who growled from his corner of the room. "Who is it?"

"Police!" The door rattled on its hinges under someone's fist. "Open up!"

Bolan shot Cervantes a look, and she quickly whispered into her throat mike. The agent shook her head. Satellite surveillance and radio traffic showed no law-enforcement units in the area.

"We have a warrant! Open up!"

Bolan nodded again at Lyons, who snarled angrily, "Just a damn minute!" Lyons turned on the bedside lamp and sighted down the barrel of his shotgun.

"Open up now, or we break it down!"

"I'm coming!" Lyons shouted.

Bolan silently counted three and raised his baseball cap in front of the peephole. The moment the hat eclipsed it, the cap, the peephole and a section of the door around it shredded away with the blast of a shotgun.

Lyons's scattergun detonated in instant answer and punched a dozen holes through the door at chest level. His second blast pierced the door at knee level. From the hall, someone screamed as they caught a part of the pattern of lead buckshot.

Bolan put his foot into the beleaguered door and kicked it off the hinges. The door flew into the face of a gunman with a revolver in each hand. The gaping hole where the peephole had been fell around the assassin's neck like a stock. Bolan punched a 3-round burst through the door as the assassin flailed his pistols around the edges ineffectually. The Executioner whirled and shot at a machete-armed assassin with each pistol. The six 9 mm hollowpoint bullets lifted the killer onto his toes and dropped him limp to the faded carpeting.

Bolan spun.

A man was hopping down the hallway. One leg hung limp, Chinos spattered with blood from Lyons's buckshot. The Beretta snarled in Bolan's left hand and swept the assassin's remaining leg out from under him. Bolan stalked down the hall as the gangster cried out and fell. He raised his foot and brought it down on the killer's gun hand, shattering the small bones and eliciting a scream. Bolan kicked the gun away and moved for the stairs. "Carl, with me! Candy! Watch the fire escape!"

Bolan charged the stairwell with Lyons on his heels. "Where's my Glock, Control?"

"In the building," Price replied.

Bolan kicked the door to the stairs. He dropped to one knee as an M-16 rifle sent a 3-round burst from the second-story landing into the ceiling. Bolan put his front sights on the rifleman's chest and squeezed both triggers. The six rounds slammed into the ambusher's chest and slapped him down the stairwell in a tangle of limbs.

"Striker! This is Control! Your Glock just left the building out the back!" Price's voice said.

"Suspects in sight, Striker! Two of them!" Cervantes's voice came over the link, shouting over the sound of her submachine gun. "They're ignoring the van and going for a blue Cadillac!"

Bolan and Lyons took the stairs three at a time. Residents of the hotel were screaming on all floors. Someone had pulled the fire alarm, and the rusted sprinklers overhead wheezed and began spritzing water. Bolan hit the ground floor. The old man behind the front desk was shouting into the phone to the police. He shrieked as Bolan vaulted the desk followed by Lyons.

The men charged down a narrow hall cluttered with wheeled laundry bins. The back door was open, and from the alley beyond it sounded like a battle was taking place. Bolan made out the short, controlled bursts from Cervantes's MP-5. A shotgun boomed like a cannon in response. Bolan heard the unmistakable snarl of a Glock 18C ripping off an entire nineteen round magazine at twelve hundred rounds per minute.

One of his birds had come home to roost.

The Executioner entered the alley with a machine pistol in each hand. The blue Cadillac was parked a dozen yards away. Its engine popped and ticked in its final death throes. Steam rose up from the holes in the hood where Cervantes had burned an entire magazine into the engine block. The man with the machine pistol dropped behind the car as his weapon clacked open on empty. The man with the pump shotgun was sighting up at Cervantes.

Bolan burned him down with a burst from both Berettas. The Executioner stalked forward, weapons rolling in his hands. The car's windshield burst apart, and the rearview mirror was shot away in Bolan's onslaught. Lyons cycled his shotgun on semiauto, and the vehicle began to come apart. The crouching man burst from cover in a desperate flight for freedom. The Glock pistol in his hand was still racked open on empty. Bolan dropped his Berettas and sprinted down the alley after him. The gangster made the fatal mistake of looking back, and he screamed as he saw the Executioner overtaking him.

Bolan hit him with a flying tackle. He ducked his head and let the gangster take the impact as they flew into a trash container with bone-jarring force. The Executioner rolled on top and stiffened his hand into a blunt ax. He chopped the knife-edge of his hand into the man's temple, and the gangster's eyes glazed with the impact. Bolan pulled the gangster up by the front of his shirt and slammed him up against the wall. He stared at Bolan in a stunned horror of recognition.

Bolan's smile was as cold as death. "Hello, Tuco."

FBI Headquarters, Washington, D.C.

BOLAN, LYONS AND Cervantes stared at Tuco through the one-way mirror. The gangster sat in an interrogation room looking miserable. The entire left side of his face was a misshapen black-and-blue lump where Bolan had hit him. A pair of FBI gang unit specialists explained the facts of life to Tuco in English and Spanish.

Bolan's death was all over the morning news. The security agent who had heroically saved Judge MacNight's life had been slaughtered in a horrific gunfight. The police were still looking for leads. A description and sketch of Tuco was circulating in the newspapers and on television.

The FBI agents explained that Tuco's situation was very simple. They could convict him on arms trafficking, possession of automatic weapons, conspiracy to commit murder and multiple counts of attempted murder, including that of a federal agent. The deal was Tuco would contact his superiors in the D.C. area and ask to be brought in, and Tuco was going to wear a wire.

A short, black agent named Tompkins left the interrogation room and joined Bolan and his party. He didn't look happy at all. "Well, we offered him your deal, and he's agreed."

Bolan nodded sympathetically. "But you're not buying it."

Tompkins shook his head. "I consider him an extreme flight risk. You let him go, and he is gone."

"I'm banking on it," Bolan said.

The FBI agent looked angry. "Listen, I'm not just talking going underground, I mean, he's gone, like out of D.C. and probably out of the country. Unlike other gangs, Mara Salvatrucha members don't necessarily stick to any particular territory. They migrate like birds. When the heat's on, they're gone. We have his fingerprints, but once he flees, he'll just be one more Hispanic male illegal out of millions in the U.S. And that's if he stays. Most flee across the border into Mexico."

"That's right, but Tuco knows something is up. He'll disappear, all right, but so that he can go and report to his superiors. I'm thinking probably Los Angeles," Bolan said.

"The first thing his people will do is check him for a wire. He'll rip it off and run first chance he gets."

"I'm counting on that, too."

Tompkins rolled his eyes. "Listen, unless you can magically track him by satellite—"

"Actually, I can," Bolan stated.

Tompkins just stared. "Really."

"Yeah. Tuco is part of the team now." Bolan glanced back through the glass at the handcuffed gangster in the cell. "Give him back his gun."

5

Los Angeles

"They let you go?" Lupo Montego stared at Tuco emotionlessly. "The FBI? Just like that?"

Tuco flinched under Montego's unforgiving gaze. Lupo Montego was a very large man. His wide, almond-shaped eyes, flat features, hooked nose and thick, permanently scowling lips revealed a great deal of Indian blood in his ancestry. He eyed Tuco with about as much sympathy as the stone carving he resembled. He had been sent from El Salvador two years earlier to make sure things ran smoothly.

He was not amused by the growing fiasco in D.C.

Tuco glanced around the stockroom of the supermarket nervously. Four local boys lounged against crates, waiting for Montego to order Tuco's dismemberment. A machete gleamed where it had been chopped into a crate. "They wanted me to wear a wire. To give up the D.C. cliques," he said.

Tuco had been given a full body search and was clean, but Montego was still suspicious. "Where is the wire now?"

"Down a toilet, back in D.C."

"You say this guy, the one who sold you the guns, is the same guy who wiped out your homies in D.C.?"

"Yes, Lupo, it was him, and the scary dude with him, the blondie. There was someone else in the room, too, but I didn't see them. It was an ambush, Lupo." Tuco shrugged helplessly. "They had machine guns."

"These two Americans, you do not think they were FBI?"

"No way they were cops." Tuco shuddered as he remembered the swiftness of the ambush and the brutality of the counterattack. "They acted more like soldiers."

"And there is no way they could have followed you?"

"I went from D.C. to L.A. through your pipeline, Lupo. I don't see how."

Montego scowled at the implication. He knew no one had followed Tuco. He had four men dead and six in the hospital. Dead men told no tales, and the Feds could grill the injured men until doomsday before they would talk. They would take their jail sentences and become part of Mara Salvatrucha's web of prison gangs. Tuco was a different story. He had been caught and then escaped under very troubling circumstances. However, Tuco had shot and killed a police officer in San Salvador and another in Portland, Oregon, to earn his leader status among the D.C. cliques. In D.C., he'd proved he had the brains to both recognize criminal opportunities and act on them. Tuco was hard-core MS to the bone. The only two things on God's green Earth Tuco feared were being deported back to El Salvador, and Lupo.

"They'll have a warrant out for you," Montego said.

Tuco nodded vigorously. "Get me to Mexico."

Montego did not immediately address Tuco's request. "They still have our money and drugs."

Tuco played his only card. "We still have their guns."

One of Montego's caterpillar-like eyebrows raised. "We do?"

"All fifty."

"Where?"

"They are on a truck, on their way here right now."

Montego shook his head. "The Feds will have the serial numbers. They'll be waiting for them to turn up."

"Not in Mexico," Tuco suggested hopefully. "Certainly not in San Salvador."

"Are they good?"

Tuco sagged inwardly with relief. The meeting had ceased being a trial. Now it was business. "They are special." Tuco nodded at his gym bag in the corner. One of Montego's men scooped it up and brought it to Tuco. He unzipped the bag and pulled out the Glock 18C.

Montego barely nodded his massive head. "Glocks are good."

"Check it, Lupo." Tuco aimed the pistol at a twenty-pound bag of rice. He pressed the button and the laser dot appeared on the bag. Tuco quoted Bolan word for word. "Where the dot goes? The bullets go. Where the bullets go…?" Tuco pointed at the slide. You see the lever? You flick it. It's a machine gun."

The collected Mara Salvatrucha members grinned. Tuco reached into the bag and pulled out a second Glock. He set the pistol on the little table between them. "My gift to you, Lupo. Thank you for bringing me in, and listening to me."

Montego took the pistol with an almost imperceptible nod of thanks. He pressed the laser switch and concealed his childlike delight as he played the beam over a pallet of flour.

"And please, Lupo—" Tuco pulled out a third Glock and put it on the table "—tell Franco my side of the story. It was a federal sting. Tell him I don't know what else I could have done, and please, give him this pistol, with my compliments."

Montego turned to one of his men. "Chinchin, call Moses. Tell him I want Tuco across the border, tonight."

Montego tucked a Glock under his jacket and handed the other to one of the men behind him. "Tuco, once you're in Mexico, Moses will set you up with some money and transportation. You're gonna go to Coahuila."

Tuco sighed with relief. "What's in Coahuila, Lupo?"

A rare smile came to Montego's face. "Oh, we got a *big* job in Coahuila."

"A GLOCK JUST CROSSED the border." Carl Lyons sat with a laptop across his knees. Cables snaked from it to a portable satellite link on the hotel floor. He watched dots move across the North American map on the screen. "One is still here in L.A. The third just went airborne out of LAX."

"What about the main consignment of guns?" Bolan asked.

"Numbers four through fifty crossed the Arizona border an hour ago. They're on a semi heading westbound on Interstate 10 straight for Los Angeles."

"What's the address on the one here?" Bolan asked.

Candy Cervantes typed on her laptop. She was linked to the FBI central server. "Oh, we know this one. Martin 'Lupo' Montego."

"What's his story?"

"The Wolf? He's bad medicine. L.A. is his territory, but he's been to D.C. three times in the past two years, and every time people dropped like flies. He's a chief. Judge, jury and executioner all rolled into one. Hold on a sec." Cervantes hit keys, and Montego's mug shot and rap sheet appeared on Bolan's laptop. "There's your boy."

Bolan took in the brutal countenance and a long list of crimes. He had been arrested for rape, murder, conspiracy, smuggling and a host of felonies. But there were only two misdemeanor convictions. Bolan noted the irony. One had been a concealed weapon charge.

Lyons looked up. "You want to go take him down?"

"No, not just yet. Sooner or later, they're going to figure out the guns are tagged. I want those Glocks to see some distribution before we move on them, and I want to get a look at who Lupo talks to."

THE SYRIAN WAS APPALLED. He was blade thin and wore a tropical weight, blue wool suit designed and exquisitely tailored to his frame in Paris. He sat on a sagging couch in the rotting tenement sipping coffee and tried not to touch anything. His companions lounged about in tracksuit bottoms or Chinos. In the summer heat, they wore sleeveless T-shirts or no shirts at all. Tattoos covered nearly every inch of their exposed bodies.

The Syrian's appointed bodyguard-chauffeur in Los Angeles was a man named Gato. A tattooed scene of the Crucifixion took up Gato's entire chest. The Syrian felt disgusted. He considered himself a devout Muslim and he found the Christians obsession with graven idols and the crucifix utterly revolting.

One of the gangsters spoke into his phone and grunted at his guest. "Lupo is here."

A crackhead out in the hall yelped as he was kicked out of the way. Montego walked into the room. He was accompanied by two of his men and a redheaded man with a beard and a mustache who wore a charcoal gray suit and carried himself like the professor he was.

The Syrian rose and took the man's hand. He allowed himself a small smile as he spoke in French. "It is good to see you, Doctor."

"And you, Ali," the redhead replied.

"All is in readiness?"

"Everything is going according to plan."

"They do not suspect?" the Syrian asked.

The man grinned disarmingly. "These pricks have no idea what they are in for."

The gang members looked back and forth between the two men. Montego stared at the two men with a frightening intensity. "What the fuck are you two talking about?"

The Syrian sighed patiently. "We studied French at school together."

Montego spent several stone-faced moments internalizing this. "Don't ever fucking do it again. I'll kill you."

The Syrian bowed. "Of course."

The professor just kept smiling.

BOLAN WATCHED MONTEGO and his companions enter the tenement. "Bear, we got anything yet?"

"Not yet, the pics you sent of the redhead are good, but he's not coming up on any databases," Kurtzman said over the secured phone line.

From his spot in the surveillance van Bolan had

noted the cut of the man's suit. It looked English, was entirely too heavy for L.A. in summer and absolutely out of place in this neighborhood. Bolan's instincts told him the man had just gotten off a plane. "This guy isn't local. Check Interpol files." The soldier noted the red hair. "Run it by MI-6 and see if he turns up IRA. That guy has no business here except bad business. I want LAX security camera tapes for the last six hours of incoming international flights."

"I'm on it."

Carl Lyons frowned at the broken windows of the rundown building. "Unless they brought that guy here to get laid or smoke crack, they're meeting somebody."

Bolan glanced down the street. A pair of kids no older than twelve sat on the curb playing a handheld video game. They wore expensive sneakers and both had cell phones clipped to their tracksuits. They were paid lookouts, pure and simple.

"I want to go in there and have a look."

Bolan turned to Cervantes. "You ready to tart it up again?"

Cervantes sighed and began changing into her prostitute regalia.

Bolan changed into a suit and donned sunglasses. The two of them slipped out of the van and approached the distracted lookouts.

"C'mon baby!" Cervantes grabbed his hand. "I don't got all day!"

Bolan watched from behind his shades as the two twelve-year-old gangbangers took notice of him from the next stoop. He looked exactly like a white boy on the wrong side of town looking to get a little something that he couldn't get at home. The lookouts would figure he was about to get rolled or have the time of his life. If they called anybody, it wouldn't be Montego but their local gang leader to tell him a new hooker was working their street. They stared at Bolan with detached hostility as he skulked past them, following Cervantes into the building.

The rotting tenement was the last stop for L.A.'s bottom rung. Among the transients and the squatters, the lines between junkie and drug dealer, prostitute and pimp blurred from moment to moment and fix to fix. Bolan knew Mara Salvatrucha was the alpha predator, controlling the flow of crack.

A young man with the sunken eyes and a pallor of the undead lay on a filthy sofa inside an open room. The junkie cringed and exposed the rotten teeth of a crack smoker in a shaky smile. "Hey, man," he said, spotting Bolan and Cervantes.

Bolan produced his Beretta machine pistol. "Where's Lupo?"

The young man pointed to the ceiling.

"Get out," Bolan said gruffly.

The junkie scuttled away.

Bolan and Cervantes entered and closed the door behind them. The Executioner checked the layout of the room. He needed to do a recon of the room above. He went to the broken radiator and pulled over a rickety dresser missing all but one of its drawers. "Drill."

Cervantes reached into her oversized bag and pulled out a laptop and a hand auger. The dresser creaked as it took Bolan's weight, and he slowly began boring a tiny hole through the ceiling.

Cervantes connected a flexible camera stalk cable to the computer and then handed the camera to Bolan. He snaked it up through the hole and felt it clear into the room above. The people above would be on a fairly high state of alert, but he doubted any of them would be watching the floor between the radiator pipes.

Cervantes held up the laptop as Bolan panned the tiny camera around the room. There were eight men directly above them. "There's Lupo, there's the white boy, there's one ugly ass dog, and..." Cervantes frowned. "Who's that?"

Bolan took in an acerbic looking Middle Eastern man sitting on the couch. "Don't know. Bear, you getting this?"

Kurtzman's voice came back. "I have a clear picture. Hold on."

In Virginia the cybernetic system was running the camera capture of the man against thousands of FBI, CIA and Interpol file photos. "Got him! Transmitting."

An inset appeared on the laptop screen. Cervantes's eyes widened. "God damn..."

The man was Ali Nur-Hadj. The Syrian was wanted by the United States, Iraqi and Israeli governments. He specialized in organizing and training insurgents in the use of improvised explosives. His operations had varied from assisting suicide bombers coming across the Israeli-Palestinian border to arming and assisting insurgents in roadside and car bombings in Iraq. That such a man was taking a meet with one of Mara Salvatrucha's main go-to guys in the U.S. was a very disturbing question.

"Ironman, this is Striker. The situation has changed. We're going in hard. Prepare for tear gas and flashbangs. I want prisoners."

"Affirmative, Striker," Lyons came back. "I've got the back door."

Bolan panned and scanned, trying to make out if there was anyone else in the room, but his angle was bad. "All right, let's—"

Movement suddenly blurred at the edge of the camera's view. The drooling, fanged maw of a pitbull filled the camera's world. The jaws snapped shut and the screen fuzzed and went blank. The camera cable was nearly ripped from Bolan's hands as the animal savaged it. Bolan let the cable go and drew his pistol as he jumped away. "Ironman! We've been made!"

"Inbound!"

Cervantes called in the FBI backup team. She threw herself to one side as bullets ripped through the ceiling.

Bolan recognized the buzz-saw sound of an automatic Glock, then half a dozen handguns joined the din above. Bolan printed answering tribursts into ceiling. Plaster fell, the light fixture shattered and shot sparks as fire was exchanged between floors. People screamed in terror throughout the tenement.

A tracer streaked through the ceiling like a comet and slammed brutally into Bolan's collarbone. The soft body armor he wore beneath his jacket held, but white pain shot down his arm, and his right hand went numb. His Beretta clattered to the floor just as the door was kicked in.

An obese gangster filled the doorway with a machete in hand. Bolan spun, and the heel of his shoe connected with the man's face, knocking him against the wall. A second man came through the door shooting. Cervantes double-tapped him with her pistol.

The fat man came off the wall and bore into Bolan. Both hands seized the Executioner's throat as they tumbled through the doorway. They fell to the floor, and the gangster rolled on top. Fingers as thick as sausages vised on Bolan's throat. The soldier tried to gouge out his opponent's eye, but his right arm would barely obey him. He saw stars as the man bounced his skull against the filthy floor.

Bolan threw a left hand into the side of his opponent's skull, but he hunched his fleshy shoulders and the blow glanced off. Stars exploded behind Bolan's eyes as his head rebounded against the floor again. His vision began to tunnel as oxygen debt took its horrible toll. He cocked back his left hand again, opening his weakening hand for a claw strike.

Suddenly, the top of the gangster's head became a geyser. Bolan pushed the vast dead bulk of the gangster off him and rolled to his feet.

Cervantes stood with her pistol in both hands. "You all right?"

Sirens howled in the street outside. Gangsters spilled out of the stairwell. Bolan and Cervantes shot in concert. Two men fell before they knew what had happened. A third collapsed into the stairwell, screaming and clutching his face.

"You've got no way out!" Bolan forced his voice into a parade ground bellow of command. "Give it up!"

A tweed-jacketed arm snaked around the doorjamb in answer. It sent an aluminum briefcase sliding down the hallway at Bolan and Cervantes. Bolan threw a shoulder into his companion and knocked her back into the room. He dived after her as the world erupted in orange fire and thunder.

Stony Man Farm, Virginia

Aaron Kurtzman wheeled into the room. "How do you feel?"

"Better. What's the situation in L.A.?" Bolan asked.

"Well, Lupo, Nur-Hadj and your redheaded friend pulled a disappearing act. That case he threw at you had about ten pounds of C-4 in it. Satchel charge, pure and simple. After he tried to drop the building on you, they went down to the basement. They'd knocked a hole into the sewer system, and they set off a second charge to foil the FBI pursuit."

"Pretty sophisticated for street gangsters," Bolan suggested.

"Yeah, well, it looks like they've been having some consultant work done. Ali Nur-Hadj is known for blowing things up and then blowing up anyone who comes after him, as well. You're going to have to figure on any place he's been being booby-trapped," Kurtzman said.

"Where are our boys now?"

"Glock one and two are in Mexico."

"That'll be Tuco and Lupo. What part of Mexico are they in?"

"One is in the state Coahuila, near the city of Nuevo Laredo on the border. The other is heading west across Sonora in that general direction."

"What about the main consignment?" Bolan asked.

"They're still traveling together as a unit by truck. They're in Mexico and heading west as well." Kurtzman grinned. "Number three, on the other hand, landed in San Salvador last night."

"You have a name and an address?"

"No, not yet. But the CIA has a fairly extensive set of resources down there, and they're working on it. Which way are you going to go?"

Bolan had been giving that some thought. "I don't like this Nur-Hadj showing up in L.A. and having a meet with Mara Salvatrucha, and I don't know who the redhead is but I like him even less. I think something is going to go down on the border, and it's going to be bad."

Candy Cervantes walked into the room. Other than a fat lip where her face had met the floor when Bolan tackled her, she had come through the battle unscathed. She had flown back east with Bolan by private jet to debrief her superiors about the presence of Ali Nur-Hadj in Los Angeles.

"Well, where do we go from here?" she asked.

Bolan sighed. "How about I take you to Texas?"

Cervantes blinked. "I'll get my hat."

San Salvador

JESS FRANCO FONDLED the Glock. He liked the gun. He liked it a lot. For the moment, he had forgiven Tuco his trespasses, real or imagined. Nevertheless, he did not like the current state of affairs at all.

Franco was short, with a shaggy haircut, a big nose and weak chin that he failed to hide behind a sparse mustache and beard. His rumpled black suit hid acres of MS-13 ink. He had killed his first man with a machete at the age of twelve, and a single look into his disturbing black eyes would tell anyone why he was the de facto warlord of Mara Salvatrucha worldwide. And, depending who one talked to, he was considered to be the most dangerous man in El Salvador.

Franco lit one cigarette with the butt of another and gazed frankly at his guest. "You know? I do not like it."

"Neither do I." Salah Samman was a Saudi Arabian, but with his shoulder-length black hair, gold jewelry and the casual way he draped himself on the couch, he could have easily passed for a South American soap opera star. With his twinkling dark eyes and gleaming smile, one would suspect him more of modeling or appearing in toothpaste commercials rather than being a wanted terrorist.

Both the United States and Interpol wanted Samman very badly. But they knew him only by aliases and rumors, and had never obtained a picture of him. Salah Samman took a great deal of pleasure in living a life of privileged ease, killing citizens and soldiers of the United States, and hiding in plain sight in North, Central and South America.

Franco blew smoke up at the ceiling fan and distractedly played the laser sight through it. "So who are the fucking Americans following?"

Samman shrugged elegantly and spoke in perfect Spanish. "Well, my friend, they followed Tuco, Lupo, or Ali. I cannot imagine them having the slightest idea who the professor is, much less his connection with us, and I have doubts they knew Ali was in the United States."

Franco lowered the Glock. "So, you put this upon my table?"

Samman clicked open a gold lighter and lit a cigarette. He blew a smoke ring and observed it intensely as it floated upward. "I am only being logical."

Franco sighed and glanced out toward the balcony. "Soledad?"

A woman rose from where she had been sunning herself and came in through the open glass doorway. She was tall, with long, slinky limbs and prominent hipbones, clavicles and ribs. Her sharp chin and cheekbones and huge, slightly sunken eyes only added to the effect, like a vampire porn star who had missed a few meals. The Gothic effect was offset by a glowing, golden brown tan. She walked up to Samman, plucked the cigarette from between his lips and took a long drag before replacing it. Only then did she throw on a black silk robe and sprawl out upon the opposite couch.

"I agree with Salah. They followed either Tuco or Lupo. Lupo's loyalty is unquestioned. Which leads me to think Tuco. He has been a question mark in my mind since the incidents in Washington."

Franco regarded Soledad with pleasure. "Yes, but how could they be following him?"

Samman sighed. "Because he is a traitor."

"Highly unlikely," Franco said.

Samman shrugged. "All men have a price."

"Still." Franco lit himself another cigarette from the stub of the old. "I find it hard to believe."

Soni tapped on the door and stuck in his head. He was Franco's right-hand man and had been with him since the beginning. He was dapper, where Franco was a disheveled mess. Where Franco was prone to sullenness and rages, Soni smiled. He smiled widest when he killed someone. "The professor is here," he announced.

Franco nodded distractedly. "Send him in."

The professor entered the room escorted by Soni. His scholarly tweeds had been replaced by a garish Hawaiian shirt and shorts. He sat on the couch next to Soledad and took out a pipe. He grinned and spoke in respectable Spanish. "Why the long faces?"

Franco scowled at the ceiling. "Soledad and Salah think Tuco may be a traitor."

The professor puffed his pipe and bent his intellect around the problem. "I don't think he's a traitor, but I do think he is being followed. They hit him in D.C., and then again in L.A." He pointed his pipe at Franco. "Where is Tuco now?"

"He is in Mexico, in Coahuila. Lupo is on the way."

The professor quirked one red eyebrow in mild alarm. "Tuco's not at the facility, is he?"

"No." Franco shook his head. "I did not think it prudent. I told him to stay in the city."

"Good, very good." The professor sat back and smoked happily.

Soledad smiled. "You have something in mind?"

"Yes, I believe someone, probably the FBI, is following Tuco, seeing where he will go and who he will meet. Just as they followed him to Los Angeles and discovered myself and Ali. I believe it is the same man. I believe this man will follow Tuco into Mexico."

"We should kill Tuco now." Soledad's dark eyes glittered. "And wipe the trail clean."

The professor puffed his pipe. "No."

"No?" Soledad's dark eyes narrowed dangerously. She was Franco's mistress, as well as one of his most trusted advisers. She didn't like being contradicted in front of him, much less by the hired help.

Soni watched the tension between them. He didn't trust Soledad.

"No. The enemy is following him, but now they will be following him into Mexico. A place where they have no jurisdiction. I am sure, Franco, that Mara Salvatrucha has many contacts within the local police in Coahuila?" the professor asked.

"Indeed." Franco nodded.

"So, if the Americans attempt to get permission or assistance from Mexican authorities, you will know about it. Though frankly, I am willing to assume this is some kind of clandestine operation and your Yankee friend will be going 'cowboy' across the border."

A smile of appreciation ghosted across Soledad's face. "You wish to set a trap for the American and use Tuco as bait."

"Why not? He was going to die anyway."

Soni's smile lit up the room. He'd never liked Tuco.

Tuco was indeed going to die, Franco thought. A lot of people were going to die, perhaps millions. Franco did not much care about the professor or Salah's political agendas. What he cared about much more were the millions of dollars being funneled into his offshore accounts in the Caribbean.

A smile began to creep across Franco's face. "I like it. Let us set a trap for this American." His smile grew as he played the scene in his mind. "I want to capture this American alive, and anyone with him. And then I want to hear him sing like a bird beneath the machete."

Texas

Bolan crossed the Rio Grande. Special Agent Candelaria Cervantes wore a black cowboy hat. Bolan wore a specially tailored blue guayabera shirt, all-terrain sandals and a pair of khaki shorts with a few extra pockets both overt and concealed.

The enemy thought they were playing hide-and-seek.

The Executioner was playing seek-and-destroy.

He glanced at his highly modified wristwatch. The dials were all fully functional, but as he turned the bezel, the dials began turning as the computer chip within began telling him his direction and distance from the tagged Glock.

Tuco was in Nuevo Laredo.

Bolan stepped off the ferry. The valet rolled the black, supercharged 1968 Chevrolet El Camino down the ramp. The 400 horsepower engine rumbled in idle as the valet reluctantly left the cockpit of tinted windows and black on black interior. Anything on the Chevy that wasn't midnight black was gleaming chrome. "Nice car, *señor.*"

Bolan gave him a ten-dollar bill. "Thanks." He opened the door for Cervantes. The FBI agent climbed in and shook her head at the muscle car surrounding her.

"We're undercover? In this?"

"Mexico is a macho culture." Bolan gunned the massive engine. People all around the dock turned to look as the gleaming dinosaur roared out in challenge. "And I never said we were undercover."

The Executioner rumbled through the streets of Nuevo Laredo. They passed the bright lights of the restaurants, hotels and casinos by the river and turned inland down the strip past the bars and nightclubs with high-rises scraping the sky behind them. The city quickly gave way to suburbs, where the well-to-do lived in large houses surrounded by high walls strung with barbed wire. In the blink of an eye, they were in the slums.

As they passed through the streets, heads looked up. As they drove deeper and deeper into the slums, more and more of the signs were the *M* and *S* of Mara Salvatrucha.

"I think we're getting close," Cervantes suggested.

Bolan checked the dials on his watch. "Actually, I think we're heading out of town."

The El Camino wound through the barrios to the shanties of the desperately poor, then civilization suddenly ceased and they were in the wilderness. They followed the dusty road across grassland that had turned brown with the summer heat. Nearly every hundred yards, a small shrine to one saint or another stood by the side of the road like milestones. An army of mice scampered in blind panic across the road followed by a writhing horde of small snakes.

Bolan saw lights up ahead and killed his own. He and Cervantes pulled on night-vision goggles and drove as stealthily as the rumble of the big Chevy would allow. He pulled up the dirt drive to the low-ceilinged adobe buildings. His watch told him the Glock was directly ahead and within one hundred yards. Satellite recon said that the pistol had been in this location for the past seventeen hours.

Bolan took in the target.

The front wall was a faded mural of a half-naked woman in a torn Mexican peasant dress swathed by half a dozen rattlesnakes. Hoyo de la Serpiente was painted over the door. The Snake Pit was a roadhouse, pure and simple. A line of pickup trucks of various makes was parked outside the cantina. A very large man stood in front of the door smoking a cigarette. He squinted into the darkness at the sound of Bolan's approaching vehicle.

Bolan parked and left the engine running. "Get out first. Go chat up the bouncer," he said.

Cervantes jumped out and put a wiggle in her walk for the doorman.

Bolan slid out the driver's side silently and made an oblique approach while the big man was distracted.

Cervantes was speaking rapid Spanish, and claimed to have been sent for by Tuco. The bouncer's eyes roved up and down the woman's curves, but he kept shaking his head. Bolan couldn't catch all the words, but the bouncer clearly hadn't been given any word about anyone ordering out for women. He took out his cell phone.

The soles of Bolan's sandals made no noise on the clay porch as he came in from the side. The bouncer's head snapped around in shock as he became aware of Bolan.

Cervantes brought the toe of her cowboy boot up between the bouncer's legs, and he fell to his knees, clutching himself in agony. The knife-edge of Bolan's right hand chopped into the back of the man's bull-like neck and ended his suffering. The Executioner stepped over the unconscious doorman and kicked open the cantina door.

The Snake Pit was dimly lit, with a small stage. There were no women working the stage or the cantina. Instead there were two dozen men armed with M-16s and AK-47s who stared in surprise as the door flew open.

Tuco shouted in Spanish. "That's him! That's—"

Bolan ripped open his shirt and drew steel from both

shoulder holsters. The Beretta 93-R banged once as he shot Tuco in the shoulder. Bolan flicked the safety off the cocked and locked Desert Eagle.

The Executioner shot the first two riflemen who got up out of their seats, then retreated back through the door with both pistols rolling and spitting fire in his hands. He spun to one side of the door as half a dozen rifles roared in response.

Agent Cervantes stared incredulously.

"No one in there but bad guys, and we were expected." He reholstered his weapons and strode to the El Camino.

"What the hell are you doing?" Cervantes asked.

"Giving Tuco a couple of seconds to bolt. Cover the door."

Cervantes began firing her Smith & Wesson through the door. Bolan flipped the latches on the car's bed cover and pulled out a USAS-12 semiauto shotgun. He snapped a 20-round drum into place, racked the action and flicked the selector to burst mode.

"Jesus, what are you going to—"

"All right, Tuco!" Bolan's voice boomed out at parade ground decibels. "You called down the thunder! Well, now you've got it!"

The South Korean shotgun began detonating in Bolan's hands. He sent five rounds smashing through the shutters of both front windows and sent ten straight through the door. Inside the Snake Pit, thunder sounded.

Incandescent lightning flashed blindingly with every report through the shattered windows and the door like a strobe light.

The weapon locked open on empty, and Bolan ejected the spent drum and snapped in a 10-round magazine of buckshot. He looped the sling over his shoulder. "Cover my six."

Cervantes followed as the Executioner strode into the snake's den.

The Mara Salvatrucha hardmen were in a bad way. The 12-gauge Flash Thunder Grenade Ammo had gone off in an enclosed space. No one inside had been spared the 182 decibels of sound and 2,000,000 candle-power of light, and they had taken the sensory assault twenty times in the space of three seconds. Thousands of winking sparks fluttered and drifted in a cloud of disorienting, pyrotechnic after-effect. Half of the men were down, and the ones standing were temporarily blinded, deafened and staggering like drunks.

Bolan noted that Tuco was nowhere to be seen.

The cantina was silent save for the moans of the wounded.

The bartender slowly rose with his hands empty and in the air. He stared around at the score of Mara Salvatrucha men littering the floor in horror.

"What's your name?" Bolan asked.

"Raoul," the man said.

He screamed as Bolan spun his shotgun on its sling

and began firing. The bartender flinched and shrieked as Bolan unloaded into the bar above and to either side of him. Whiskey, tequila and gin bottles exploded, and the mirror shattered under the onslaught of lead. The Executioner dropped the smoking weapon on its sling. "Raoul, you tell Tuco I want his ass. Tell him it's personal. Tell him I won't stop coming. Ever."

Bolan pulled off the Nuevo Laredo strip and parked behind a little town house. He grabbed the gear from the back and walked up the dark narrow stairs. His fist pounded on the door in the arranged signal. Carl Lyons opened the door with a loaded .357 in his hands. "Hey, Striker."

"How's our boy Tuco?"

"He beat it for the hills. Satellite recon has two of our Glocks converging on him. How'd it go on your end?"

Bolan handed Lyons his massive shotgun. "Worked like a champ."

A rare smile passed across Lyons's face. The Machine Gun Stun technique was his own invention, and one he was rather proud of.

The laptop on the little desk was connected to a satellite link. Bolan shed his armament onto the bed and gazed at the screen. "What Glock numbers do we have?"

"Nine and twenty-two," Lyons said.

Cervantes tossed down her bags. "Neither one of those is Lupo."

"No," Bolan agreed. "Lupo's probably laying low. These two guys are new. I'm betting they were flown in from El Salvador to solve some of the current problems. They were given the Glocks by whoever is controlling things in Central America."

Cervantes watched the dots on the screen. "They're hitters."

"They're problem solvers, dependable and expendable, and they'll be carrying machetes as well as guns." Bolan watched as the three dots converged in an area up in the hills about twenty miles outside of Nuevo Laredo. "Tuco's in a lot of trouble. I dropped a giant punk card at his feet. He won't be able to pick it up, and he won't be talking himself out of this one."

San Salvador

FRANCO WAS FURIOUS. He sat by his swimming pool and grew angrier by the second. The Turkish tobacco he smoked was bitterness in his mouth. "Twenty men?" He barely concealed his rage as he spoke into his secure phone.

"Yes," Montego confirmed.

"You told me those men were veterans! Guerrilla fighters from the war! Men you picked personally. You assured me, Lupo! You fucking assured me!"

Montego kept his nervousness out of his voice. "The bouncer confirms there was a woman who acted as a diversion. I believe she is the same woman from Los Angeles. I think she is a U.S. federal agent. The bartender, who I questioned rigorously, says the man threw in some kind of grenades. He said it was like the end of the world. Everyone was blinded and deafened... stunned, he said. He says they're after Tuco. The American said it was personal and that he would never stop coming."

"Tuco's turning into a big pain in my ass!" Franco screamed.

"The American shot Tuco through the shoulder, but he got away."

"Got away?" Franco's voice rose to a shriek. "That's awfully fucking convenient, Lupo!"

"I found that interesting, too. However, Tuco did not get away from Javier and Lucio," Montego said.

Franco took a deep breath. "Oh?"

"Do you have your laptop? Check your e-mail."

Franco flipped open his laptop. He found an e-mail message that was simply a link to a Web site. He clicked on it and nodded to himself as he began clicking on jpegs. "Hmm...yes." There was a picture of Tuco tied over a sawhorse in an empty room. He had clearly been shot through the shoulder. In the next picture, Tuco was missing his right hand. The next his left, and finally his head.

"He was questioned?" Franco asked.

"Javier and Lucio say they questioned Tuco...extensively."

"And?"

"He denied betraying us, but that proves nothing."

"So, either he betrayed us, or he was incompetent."

"Either way, he's gonna be washing up on the riverfront tomorrow morning."

"So, the trail is cold."

"I believe so," Montego said.

Franco stubbed out his cigarette. "Step up the timetable. We move in forty-eight hours."

Nuevo Laredo Coroner's Office

CERVANTES WENT a little green around the gills. "Old Tuco's not looking so good."

Bolan examined the body on the tray. Normally, identifications were made through fingerprints or dental records. That was difficult when the cadaver was missing both hands and its head. A night in the Rio Grande hadn't helped much, either. Catastrophic blood loss and bloating had turned the body into a fishbelly-white balloon. But the acres of ink covering Tuco's corpse were as good as fingerprints and exactly matched the file photos of his Mara Salvatrucha tattoos taken while he was in FBI custody. Bolan recognized the hole he'd put in the man's shoulder.

The Executioner flipped open his phone. "Ironman, how are we doing on signals?"

"It's a goddamn Glock convention just east of here. "I got Lupo, I got your two shooters. I got Tuco—"

"Tuco's dead and I'm looking at him. Someone else has the piece now."

"Good, I never liked him," Lyons said.

Bolan couldn't quite be sure if Lyons was joking or serious. "Any more?"

"Two, and they came back up from El Salvador. By the way, according to Gadgets, we have about four days left of battery time, and then we're going lose the signal."

Bolan was all too aware of the time crunch. "That's why we're going to hit them tonight."

"I was hoping you'd say that."

"Where are the signals coming from now?"

"Satellite imaging has them in the hills about fifty miles out of town. Used to be a cattle ranch and slaughter yard. They got bought out a year ago. According to the Nuevo Laredo chamber of commerce, some group wants to build a golf course and casino on the land, but it's lain fallow for the past year."

"But someone's there now," Bolan said.

"We have six of our Glock signals, and satellites show trucks, cars, horses and human inhabitants, varying from two to three dozen over the past twelve hours."

"I want to insert by air. How soon can Jack be in Mexico?"

"He's at the airstrip now," Lyons came back. "I figured we might need him."

"I'll see you in an hour. We're going in hard. Full war loads."

"They'll be ready. Ironman, out."

"So..." Cervantes eyed Bolan. "You're launching an airborne operation in Mexico."

"Yeah, you got your jump wings?"

Cervantes recoiled slightly. "Uh...no."

"No problem." Bolan waved a dismissive hand. "We'll go tandem."

PROFESSOR DRAYTON GAZED at his masterpiece. The twenty-four cylinders were stacked in a pyramid on a pallet inside the abandoned slaughterhouse. Each cylinder contained an 82 mm mortar bomb, and each one bore the universal yellow warning sticker for hazardous materials with CHEMICAL DANGER printed in huge letters below it.

Montego handed Tuco's Glock to Drayton. "Franco wanted you to have it."

The Irishman took the machine pistol and tucked it under his belt. "Thanks, Lupo."

Montego grinned at the pallet and its contents. "Death is coming to Texas."

"Oh, indeed," Drayton agreed.

"Nerve gas, huh?" Montego knew very little about chemical weapons, but he was excited about the plan. He was even more excited about the millions they were getting from the Arabs. "I hear that shit kills you dead, man. Like a bug spray."

"Oh, faster, and far worse," the Irishman said, nodding. "If it even touches your skin, you seize up, shit yourself, do the herky-jerky and die. It takes only a tiny bit, and it takes only a few seconds. It's colorless, odorless, you never know it's there. However…"

Montego's eyes widened slightly as Drayton paused. "However what?"

"Well…" Drayton continued mysteriously, "some victims who survived claim to have smelled a scent like fresh-cut grass right before the convulsions set in." Drayton lifted his chin and sniffed at the air. "Lupo? Do you smell something?"

"Shit! Hey—" Montego jumped back from the pallet. A snarl split his face. "That shit's not funny, man!"

Drayton shrugged. "Sorry."

"You wanna play with me?" Montego loomed over the Irishman. "I'll shove that pistol up your sorry ass."

Drayton smiled. "My apologies, Lupo."

Montego spit on the bloodstained floor and stomped off. Drayton watched him go, grinning. He waited until the Salvadoran had slammed the door behind him and then flipped open the latches on the top two canisters. He took out the teardrop shape of an 80 mm mortar bomb. Drayton took hold of his pride and joy by the contact fuse in the nose and turned it clockwise until it clicked three times. He then took the tailfin assembly and turned it counterclockwise until it clicked three times as well.

The weapon was armed.

The timer was set and containment would be lost in twenty-four hours. He performed the same operation on the highly modified weapon's twin and reracked them. The two bombs did not contain nerve gas. Two of the bombs beneath them did, and they had remote detonators buried within them that were linked to Drayton's cell phone. The other twenty munitions were simply standard mortar bombs that had been remarked. Standard, save that rather than contact fuses, they, too, had been modified with remote detonators.

All in all, it was a very dangerous pallet.

Drayton was satisfied. Montego had been correct. Death was coming to Texas. Death was also coming to Los Angeles, Washington, D.C., and New York. Death would probably spread its black cloak over a decent chunk of the Earth. Not that Drayton cared in the slightest about collateral damage, much less worldwide catastrophe.

The important thing, he thought, was that the United States was going to be death central. Ground zero. Drayton considered the men he was working with. They all considered themselves so self-importantly bad, so dangerous. The FBI considered Mara Salvatrucha the most dangerous gang in the United States.

Drayton laughed aloud. They, like a significant portion of the planet's population, would soon cease to exist.

The Irishman rose, checked his watch, checked the

signal strength of his cell phone and checked the loads in his new Glock.

It was time to get the hell out of Dodge.

"One minute, Sarge." Jack Grimaldi was Stony Man Farm's ace pilot. At fourteen thousand feet, the black Super Twin Otter aircraft was invisible and inaudible to everyone on the ground as it flew through the clear night air. Bolan slid open the door, and the wind whistled into the cabin. Cervantes cringed. She was spooned against Bolan's belly and held in place by the straps of the tandem jump rig, but her body posture made it very clear that she found the situation anything but intimate. Her two hours of ground school had gone badly. Cervantes was afraid of heights. As tough as she was, nothing in the FBI agent's background had prepared her for jumping out of a plane at night. Bolan was tempted to unhook her, but he needed her language and intelligence skills, and she had already proved herself in a gunfight.

Lyons yanked on their rig, testing the straps and buckles and gave Bolan the thumbs-up.

Bolan leaned into the woman's ear and spoke over the howling wind. "You down for this?"

"I think I'm going to throw up!"

"Do it now! I don't want that flying up in my face while I'm steering!"

Cervantes hunched miserably and grimly held on to her dinner. She stared at the dark expanse of Mexico nearly three miles below her and glanced back at Bolan with a despairing moan. "I hate you."

Bolan nodded. "I get that a lot."

"Go! Go! Go!" Grimaldi shouted.

Bolan jumped. Cervantes shouted in terror as she tumbled out into space with him. Carl Lyons leaped into the void right behind them. Bolan arched his body hard to stabilize their free-fall. The night was perfect for a combat jump. The sky was clear, but there was no moon. The stars over Mexico were brilliant and the Milky Way made a silver ribbon across the sky, but Bolan's attention was fixed on the lights below them. Nuevo Laredo was a blob of light to the east, and lights of towns and villages along the Rio Grande made their own ribbon across the darkened land.

Bolan and Cervantes fell through space.

Their target was clear in his night-vision goggles. Cattle pens, corrals and miles of barbed wire stretched out from the central hub of an old Spanish hacienda.

"Landing zone is the slaughter pen, Ironman. Pull at one thousand."

Lyons spoke into his radio somewhere above them. "Affirmative, Striker. LZ slaughter pen confirmed, opening at one thousand feet."

Bolan watched the altimeter on his wrist and pulled his ripcord. Cervantes made a small noise as the canopy opened and their straps cinched against them like a fist closing. Bolan took the steering toggles and began a slow, spiraling descent over the target.

"Pull up your knees," Bolan said.

He pulled on the toggles and stalled the chute. His boots hit the dust of the slaughter pen, but the chute and his partner's extra weight dragged him forward. Bolan rolled so that Cervantes wouldn't go face-first into the dust. He hit the quick-release buckles, and he and Cervantes separated. Bolan rose, while Cervantes fell to her hands and knees.

The Executioner released his jump rig and unclipped his weapon. The Colt 635 was an M-16 shortened and converted to fire 9 mm ammunition. The forearm formed an integral sound suppressor. An optical sight on top and an M-203 40 mm grenade launcher beneath the barrel completed the weapon system.

He took a knee as he scanned the perimeter. "You all right?"

Cervantes vomited into the dirt in answer.

"You did great." Bolan put a hand on her shoulder. "But we have to move."

A chute fluttered above them, and Lyons completed a textbook stand-up landing. He carried a Colt submachine gun like Bolan's, but rather than a grenade launcher he had an XM-26 Lightweight Shotgun System slaved beneath the barrel.

Cervantes ran the back of her fist across her chin and pushed herself to her feet. She unclipped her sound-suppressed Heckler & Koch SD-4 submachine gun. "We're moving."

Bolan checked his watch. According to the tracker, there were three Glock machine pistols in the hacienda. Satellite intelligence had detected traffic going in and out of the slaughterhouse for the past twelve hours, including both Tuco's and Montego's Glocks. Tuco's Glock had gone south four hours earlier. Satellite tracking had it on a flight to El Salvador. That told Bolan it was Montego and his two hitters on the scene, with a possible crew packing heat in reserve.

Bolan pointed to either side of the pen. Cervantes and Lyons took up covering positions as he crept up the slaughter chute.

Bolan crouched at the entrance. A massive padlock sealed the sheet-metal shutter. The Executioner whispered into his throat mike, "Ironman, I need a key."

Lyons loped forward like a wolf. He ejected the magazine from the abbreviated shotgun attached to his Colt and snapped in one from his web gear. He and Bolan exchanged weapons through the rail of the slaughter chute. Bolan aimed the bottom barrel of the weapon system at the padlock.

The load was a Cowboy Kissinger special. The 12-

gauge slug was bottlenecked brass rather than plastic. The silent system was as old as the tunnel rats in Vietnam. Between the slug and the propellant was a piston. When the propellant fired, the piston slammed forward into the slug, jamming against the brass shell's bottleneck and containing the expanding gas. The normal crack and muzzle-flash of a firearm stayed within the shell. The slug was propelled by kinetic energy of the piston.

Bolan squeezed the trigger.

The weapon squirmed against his shoulder with less sound than a whisper. The lead slug slammed into the top of the padlock and slapped it open. The impact made a sharp noise, and the broken padlock spun and jangled on the latch. Bolan stopped the spinning lock with his palm. Both he and his team waited long seconds for reaction, but only a coyote howled in the distance.

Bolan and Lyons exchanged weapons again. "Take lookout around front," the Executioner said.

Lyons clicked in a magazine of buckshot for maximum, close-range lethality. Bolan shoved up the steel shutter just high enough for him to enter the building in a crouch. The cavernous interior of the slaughterhouse was dark but Bolan's night-vision goggles multiplied by hundreds of times the starlight coming in the through the skylights. Meat hooks hung on chains from tracks in the ceiling. The concrete floors were stained dark with years of blood and viscera. Bolan frowned.

Planks had been laid over sawhorses to make tables, and two dozen folding chairs surrounded them. Dirty plates and empty beer bottles were scattered everywhere. The smell of alcohol and the aroma of roasted pork permeated the slaughterhouse. Bolan swept the room with the muzzle of his weapon, then motioned Cervantes forward.

The FBI agent peered about. "Someone threw a party."

Bolan nodded, but the pallet in the middle of the room held his attention. It was stacked with 80 mm mortar bomb cylinders. Bolan moved silently through the flotsam and jetsam of the fiesta. He crouched by the pyramid of bombs and played the tactical light attached to his weapon over them. The transport tubes were former Communist-block dark green, and each bore the universal bright yellow chemical warning sticker. Bolan rose. The top two cylinders were open, and he stared at the two mortar bombs.

Bolan's lips thinned. Mortar bombs didn't go off by accident. They armed themselves automatically when they were fired from their launch tube. Leaving the transport cylinders open was a shocking breech of safety protocols. Throwing a party in front of the pile was the dumbest thing Bolan had seen in a while. It was so dumb it had to be deliberate.

"Ironman, what have you got?"

"Twenty vehicles parked out front. Trucks, pickups, cars, all makes and models. No movement, Striker."

It would take just one pickup to transport the whole load. Twenty vehicles implied dispersal. "Jack, what's happening?" Bolan asked.

Grimaldi had one eye on his instruments and the other on the monitor of the Super Twin Otter's Forward Looking Infrared Radar. "No visible change of status, Sarge. You have the same two sentries at the road gate and four men walking the perimeter of the hacienda. Nothing moving within one hundred yards of you."

"What're our Glocks doing?"

"No movement in the U.S., Canada or El Salvador. They seem to be bedded down for the night."

Cervantes came up beside Bolan. "What's wrong?"

Bolan's eyes never left the pile of weapons. "That."

"You think this is a trap?"

Bolan nodded.

Cervantes stared intently at the pile of bombs. "There's no way they could have figured we were following the Glocks. Gangbangers aren't known for cleaning and field-stripping their weapons, and even if they did they wouldn't know the difference between a laser module and a tracking device."

"You're right."

"No way they knew we were coming." Her lips twisted angrily. "No way in hell there was a leak on my end. I didn't even know where we going."

Bolan spoke into his mike. "Ironman, I need you."

Bolan removed a thin black tool wallet from his web

gear. He peered under the pallet for wires or pressure plates but found nothing. He scanned the gaps between the transport cylinders and came up empty, as well.

Lyons ghosted into the slaughterhouse. "What's up?"

Bolan gestured at the closer of the two bombs. "Hold that."

Lyons stared at the bomb. "Thanks. A lot." The Ironman slowly lifted the bomb out of its cylinder and cradled it like a newborn baby.

"Candy, shine your light on it and hold it steady," Bolan said.

Cervantes shone her tactical light on the bomb. Lyons immediately scowled. "You know there's a gap between the fin assembly and the bomb housing."

Bolan had noticed. He stared long and hard at it as he took out a pair of lightweight titanium pliers. "I don't want to go in through the fuse."

"I don't want you to go in through the fuse, either," Lyons agreed.

"I'm going in through the increment." Bolan walked around Lyons to get to the back end of the bomb. Mortar bombs were very simple, and their basic design hadn't changed much in more than eighty years. You dropped the bomb down the mortar tube. Its own weight slammed it onto the firing pin at the bottom of the tube. The firing pin hit the increment, and the explosive charge at the base hurled the bomb on its merry way.

Bolan slowly began unscrewing the increment.

Lyons stood stock-still as the bomb was disassembled. The Executioner gripped the loose increment and slowly pulled it out.

"That's not good," Lyons said.

Bolan had to agree. The increment was a black cylinder the size of an old plastic 35 mm film roll. Unlike most increments, this one was trailing a red and green wire back up into the main bomb and had a small, red LED readout on the side.

"What's wrong?" Cervantes stared at the increment. "Is it going to go off?"

Bolan stared at the readout. The timer read 00.00. "It already has," he said quietly.

Cervantes recoiled. "Jesus Christ! If it's nerve gas—"

Bolan shook his head. "It's not nerve gas."

"But then it's—"

"It's a biological agent. And we've been exposed." A cold wind blew through Bolan. "So has everyone on this ranch." He thumbed his throat mike to the Stony Man Farm frequency. "Control, this is Striker."

Barbara Price answered instantly. "Striker, this is Control. What is your situation?"

"Control, we have penetrated target. Threat is believed to be biological. Nature of agent is unknown. Biological agent is not contained. Repeat, biological agent is not contained. Request immediate insertion of Delta Force. Set up one-mile perimeter around ranch, but do not allow any units to enter target area. Establish quarantine, and do not let anything inside or out. Request use of deadly force to enforce quarantine. Inform Pentagon they need to create Hot Zone Level 4 facility on this site, and inform Mexican government."

The Stony Man Farm mission controller was silent for a stunned moment. Mack Bolan had just requested an armed invasion of Mexico. "Roger, Striker, message received. Stand by."

Bolan turned to Lyons. "Carl, give me your grenades and C-4, then make your way to the front gate. No one gets past you."

Lyons put the bomb back in its cylinder, shucked off a belt of his web gear and disappeared into the night. Bolan hit his mike for Grimaldi. "Jack, maintain orbit and track anything that gets outside the ranch."

"Affirmative, Sarge."

"So…" Cervantes looked unhappily at the pallet of bombs. "You think we've been exposed to a biological agent."

"I'm almost sure of it."

"So what do we do?"

"Our job is containment." Bolan jacked a fragmentation round into his grenade launcher. "Our first priority is the vehicles." He trotted out the front door of the slaughterhouse with Cervantes on his heels. He began taking bricks of C-4 out of pockets in his web gear and pushing in remote detonator pins. Bolan tossed a brick into the open window of one of the trucks. He didn't have enough explosive to blow up every vehicle.

"Candy, start shooting out the tires on the cars."

Cervantes began firing short bursts into car tires as Bolan deployed the bricks of C-4 into the bigger vehicles.

Lyons spoke over the link. "Sentries are moving at the front of the house."

Bolan had already expected that.

"Deploying dogs," Lyons advised.

The animals came hurtling across the grounds. Their black fur turned their powerful bodies into little more than darting shadows in the darkness.

Bolan pulled Cervantes toward the slaughterhouse and pumped his detonator four times. The cabs of the two semis and two of the pickup trucks shuddered and burst as they violently gave birth to expanding balls of orange fire. The attack animals skidded and lurched as their senses were overwhelmed by the explosions. They turned in terror, heading back the way they had come.

Tracers began reaching out in smoking red lines from the hacienda. Bolan flicked up the ladder sight of his grenade launcher and sent his frag round looping up onto the portico. The grenade cracked, and men screamed as they were torn by flying fragments. Half-dressed men armed with rifles came spilling out of the hacienda. Cervantes steadfastly marched up and down the rows of vehicles blasting out tires.

"Sarge," Grimaldi radioed, "they're coming at you in platoon strength, and they aren't stopping."

Bolan considered his options. Cervantes scuttled back in a crouch. The enemy was coming on in a human wave. The Executioner let his instincts speak to him. They whispered of the deadly, unknown exposure in the slaughterhouse and the still mysterious mound of mortar bombs.

Suddenly it all became clear.

Bolan shouted loudly enough in Spanish for half of Coahuila to hear him. "Cervantes! Retreat! This way! Back inside!"

Cervantes flashed a desperate look back. She clearly preferred the lanes of vehicles and the ramble of outbuildings, going from cover to cover rather than holing up in a contaminated building. But she had learned to trust Bolan. She broke into a sprint and ran for the slaughterhouse door. Tracers streaked after her, and Bolan gave covering fire, pumping burst after burst into the mob of charging men. He ran in after her as bullets struck the corrugated wall like hail and went through it like tissue.

Cervantes turned and slammed a fresh magazine into her weapon. "I hope you have a—"

"Go!" Bolan shoved her. "Out the slaughter chute and keep going! Don't stop!"

"But they'll just—"

"Go!" Bolan roared. She went. Bolan took his last

stick of C-4 back out of its pocket and tossed it onto the pile of bombs. He heard Cervantes's boots pounding on the wooden chute outside, and he pulled his remote detonator box as he ran after her. He lunged through the door and charged down the chute. Cervantes had turned to cover him.

"Go!" Bolan shouted. The mob had reached the slaughterhouse. Half a dozen ran inside to secure the bombs while the rest forked around to either side and flanked the building as they came on. Bolan dived over a long concrete trough and rolled as bullets ripped the fence posts above. The Executioner pressed the red button on his detonator box. Inside the slaughterhouse, the stick of C-4 went off with a thump. Almost instantly, Bolan's instincts were confirmed. Mortar bomb after mortar bomb went off a like a string of firecrackers, blending into a sustained boom. The windows blasted out, and the entire structure sagged.

Cervantes was back by Bolan's side. "You all right?"

"Yeah." Bolan scanned the area over the lip of the trough. The building was falling in on itself and belching black smoke into the sky. The dead and wounded lay scattered in a circle all around it. Other gangsters ran or limped toward the hacienda.

"What do we do now?"

"The mission stays the same. Containment. No one goes in or out. The good news is they don't know how many of us are out here or that we're Americans. Now that the bombs have gone up, they'll go into siege mentality and hole up in the hacienda. When cooler heads prevail, they'll probably allow themselves to be arrested, figuring their connections on both sides of the law can get them out of it." Bolan let out a long breath. "What they don't know is that they're already dead."

"You think they were exposed to the biological agents?"

"We all were. I'm sure of it."

Cervantes fired a burst into a window where a rifleman leaned out. "But the mortar bombs, they blew up like regular bombs," she said.

"Yeah, but they're not regular bombs. The top two were the agent, but I'd bet anything the rest were all on timers as well."

"I don't get it."

Bolan kept his eyes on the hacienda. "Think about it. Twenty bombs go off across the United States. Small ones, admittedly, but the FBI would investigate. The Pentagon would send people. Those people would brief their superiors, they would brief the Joint Chiefs and the President."

"Jesus…" Cervantes got it. "And whoever planted the bombs, and wherever they planted them, in post offices, train stations, shopping malls, they'd infect everyone around them. Interviewed witnesses would infect the interrogators, they're—"

"We're the bombs," Bolan concluded. "Everyone at

this hacienda. They would have infected everyone they came in contact with as they traveled across the border and across the United States. Even if the Mexican government or the United States had swooped down and arrested everybody, the contagion would spread out of control, anyway."

"So, what do you think we're infected with?" Cervantes asked.

Bolan prepared to sit out the siege, and for what was to come. "That's the million-dollar question."

10

Carl Lyons lay naked inside a plastic tent. The U.S. Army mobile biological warfare unit formed a small city of tents on the rolling Mexican plain and surrounded the smoking ruins of the slaughterhouse and hacienda. Plastic tunnels connected the tents in a spiderweb of corridors. Lyons lay in the center of the green maze in the Hot Zone Level 4 tent. IV units hung from both sides of his bed, dripping a battery of medications and painkillers into his bloodstream. He lay unmoving save for the rise and fall of his chest. Nearly every inch of his exposed skin was lumped with raised, angry, whitecapped blemishes.

"Aren't you a little old for acne?" Bolan said.

The man's sunken eyes opened and slid sideways in their sockets to regard Bolan. "Fuck…you."

Lyons was lucky to be alive. The smallpox virus carried a thirty percent mortality rate. But for two days, Lyons had been getting stronger. Other survivors of the slaughterhouse battle were not so fortunate.

Lyons had been vaccinated against smallpox as a child. Bolan, himself, bore the vaccination scar on his left shoulder. The vaccine, however, could wear off, and exposure was a crapshoot for any vaccinated adult. It was a roll of the dice Bolan had won and Lyons had lost. No antiviral medicines were available for anyone who contracted the virus and hadn't been vaccinated. Vaccination within four days of exposure *might* prevent or lessen the effects of the smallpox, but the operating word was might. Lyons had been revaccinated within twenty-four hours and appeared to be recovering from a lesser bout of the infection.

Everyone else in the isolation unit was dead or dying.

"How's Cervantes?" Lyons croaked.

Bolan shrugged. "She's immune."

Lyons blinked.

"Well, not immune. Technically she's highly resistant. The only symptoms she's manifested have been the sniffles and a low-grade fever for two days. Chalk it up to good genetics. She's still infectious, but other than being bored she's tip-top."

"The doctors want to keep you for another week. They say you're healing fine, but they want to keep you immobile so the lesions can heal on their own without turning you into a crater face."

Lyons closed his eyes, and even that effort seemed to exhaust him.

"Sorry, big man, but you're off the case. Doctors orders," Bolan said.

"How long until Cervantes is cleared?" Lyons asked.

"Until the doctors say she's no longer infectious. They can't be sure. The virus isn't acting normally."

Lyons opened his eyes again. "So it's a weapon."

"Yeah, the virus is a strain no one's seen before. Current theory is someone got hold of some smallpox and weaponized it."

"There's your al Qaeda tie-in."

"Yeah, and our mystery man, I'm betting."

Lyons closed his eyes. For a moment, Bolan thought he'd fallen asleep. "We stopped the attack. Now you have to go after their stockpile," Lyons finally said.

"Yeah, there's been a lot of flights going back and forth from Mexico to El Salvador, and, according to Gadgets, we've got forty-eight hours or less of signal strength on the Glocks," Bolan replied.

"So you're out of here."

"Yeah. I've been cleared. I'm on a plane."

"San Salvador." Lyons sighed. "It's Dodge City down there, and you don't have a road map. How you going to play it without Cervantes?"

"Doctors think she should be cleared within the next couple of days. Until then, I'm just going to have to find another intelligence asset, preferably someone inside Mara Salvatrucha."

"And who's that gonna be?"

"I got my eye on someone."

Lyons cracked one eye open. "How you gonna draft

him to the winning team, Mack? Appeal to his humanity? These guys are Mara Salvatrucha. They don't turn."

"I'm just going to have to give him a wake-up call," the Executioner said. "Then I'm going to make him an offer he can't refuse."

"Bring in the detainee."

Two military policemen brought in a stocky, well-built young man of seventeen. He hobbled in his shackles and wore a pair of orange POW pants and prison-issue sandals. The young man wore no shirt and showed MS-13 tattoos all over his arms and torso.

Bolan sat in a sectioned-off corner of a tent behind a folding card table. The prisoner lifted his lip in a haughty sneer and spit on the floor.

Both MPs had stun guns, and they looked to Bolan for the signal to send the young man jerking and twitching to the floor.

Bolan locked eyes with the young man, who flinched under the power of the Executioner's stare.

"Unshackle him," Bolan said.

The MPs unlocked the chains around the young man's wrists, waist and ankles.

"Leave us."

The two military policemen looked at each other askance, but they had their orders. They filed out and left Bolan alone with his intelligence asset. The Executioner read the young man his rap sheet. "Guillermo

Castanado, a.k.a. 'Billy C,' El Salvadoran national, illegally in the United States, wanted for first-degree robbery and assault, carjacking, and suspected in the shooting of a California Highway Patrolman in Los Angeles. Thought to have fled California, whereabouts unknown." Bolan threw down the file. "Until now."

Castanado shrugged. "So?"

"So you're gonna help me out," Bolan said.

"Or what?"

"Or you'll die."

The young gangster blinked. Then he spread his arms wide open and sneered. "Make your move, white boy."

"Well, I haven't decided how I'm going to do it yet." Bolan shrugged. "I thought maybe I'd truss you up like a chicken and have you delivered to El Sombra Negra."

The young man flinched.

"They'd love to get their hands on a dedicated young MSer like you," Bolan said.

Castanado adopted a poker face. "I want my lawyer and my phone call, man."

"Where do you think you are?" Bolan inquired. "Who do you think I am?"

The young man suddenly seemed to realize that he was in Mexico, and the man in front of him wasn't acting like a cop. "Fuck you!" he snarled. "CIA! I spit on you! El Sombra Negra? I spit on them! I spit on all of you!" He thumped his fists into his chest and put his hands together, throwing the gang sign in Bolan's face.

"Mara Salvatrucha! For life! Forever!" He stepped back and spread his arms wide. "Make your move."

Bolan had to admit the young man was well-indoctrinated. He was loyal and had guts. He was exactly what Bolan needed. Unfortunately, the soldier was on a timetable, and he didn't have the time to set up a proper deprogramming session. Billy C was going to have to settle for a good old-fashioned Come to Jesus. The teen needed to be broken down and built back up, and the plane was leaving in an hour.

It was time for a Come to Bolan.

The Executioner pulled a folding knife out of his pocket and pressed the lever on the coffin-shaped black handle. The Mikov switchblade snapped open. Bolan stabbed the three and three-quarters inches of spear-pointed Czechoslovakian steel into the table, pushed his chair back and stood. "Make yours."

Castanado's eyes flicked back and forth between the Executioner and the killing steel between them, calculating.

Bolan nodded.

The young man lunged, but he didn't go for the knife. He went straight over the table at Bolan in a flying tackle. He was young, fast and Bolan admired his tactics.

Bolan grabbed the outstretched arms and turned, hurling Castanado in a hip throw that sent him pinwheeling into the heavy canvas of the tent wall. The teen bounced up like a jumping jack, coming straight in and screaming. Bolan couldn't afford to maim or disfigure the young man. He needed him salty for a reunion with his fellow gang members.

What was required was a lesson in pain.

Bolan swatted aside the hand clawing for his throat. His own hand clamped down like a vise on his opponent's trachea, and the young man's legs ran out from under him. Bolan heaved him up by the throat and choke-slammed the young man through the folding table. Bolan waited while the gangbanger rose from the wreckage, wheezing and stunned.

Castanado had the switchblade in his hand. "Gonna cut you, man!" he shouted, enraged.

Bolan let him take a few wild slashes at him and then ended the show. The blade flashed in Bolan's face. The Executioner leaned away from the attack. The blade had barely passed as Bolan's left fist pumped into the point of the teen's chin. His head snapped back just as Bolan's right hand buried itself into his opponent's solar plexus. He cringed and went rigid. The knife dropped from his hand. Bolan's left hand blurred in an openhanded palm strike that cracked across the young man's face like a whip, and bitch-slapped him to the ground.

Mara Salvatrucha's young lion lay on the tent floor, gasping. "You're...dead...you hear me? You're dead. Lupo's gonna kill you, man."

"Lupo?" Bolan yanked Castanado up by the hair.

"Good idea. Let's go talk to him." Bolan cranked Castanado's right arm into a hammerlock and marched him out of the tent staggering, weeping and cursing. Bolan's voice broke over his whimpers like a wave. "What did they tell you, Billy? They had their eye on you? They were looking to move you up? Had a special job for you?"

The MPs snapped to attention with their stun guns ready, but Bolan waved them away with a jerk of his head. Doctors and nurses scattered before Bolan and his captive as they marched down the tent corridor.

Bolan dragged the bleeding young man into the isolation unit. "You're only seventeen, Billy, but they gave you a top job like this? How did you earn that trust? Rumor is you shot a cop, Billy."

Bolan manhandled Castanado to a tented hospital bed and pointed at Carl Lyons. "You see him? He's a cop."

Castanado stared in uncomprehending horror at the blistered flesh of Carl Lyons. Bolan's next knife-edge chop took him in the belly and folded him to the floor. "He's my best friend."

"I didn't...I didn't...do that—"

Bolan was satisfied. The young man's innate gangster confidence had been shattered. Now it was time to introduce the crisis of faith. "I'll ask you again, Billy. Where do you think you are?"

The young man looked around in shock. "Some kinda hospital."

"Give the gangbanger a cigar." Bolan heaved him up by the hair. "Why do you think you're here? Why aren't you at Guantanamo Bay being interrogated by the FBI? Why aren't you in a cellar being tortured by the Mexican federal police?" Bolan's hand shot into Castanado's throat. "Why haven't I buried your sorry ass alive in the desert without a marker?"

Castanado dropped to his knees. Bolan yanked him up once more. "Let's ask Lupo."

Bolan shoved the young man toward to the middle of the ward and let him go. The young man was in no condition to run or fight. He wasn't going anywhere. He stood shaking as he looked at the dozen beds each covered with its own clear plastic quarantine tent. Nine of the beds were occupied.

All of them were Mara Salvatrucha members from the battle at the ranch.

The men in the tent hadn't been inoculated in their youth, so the last second vaccinations had failed them. Their bodies were covered with lesions, but theirs were hemorrhagic.

Castanado staggered forward a step. "Lupo?"

Lupo Montego lay on a bed. He was only recognizable by his size. Bleeding lesions had left the mass of Mara Salvatrucha tattoos covering his torso a bloody moonscape. His face was worse. The blisters had attacked his eyes. Lesions inside and out had turned his mouth into a slack wound.

"Now," Bolan spoke quietly, "do you know why you're here?"

"Madre de Dios..." Billy shook like a leaf as a shining new horror seized his psyche. He stared at the dying men with genuine terror. "I'm...sick?"

"No, we had to hold you until we made sure you weren't. You?" Bolan shrugged. "You're safe."

"How?"

"Figure it out, Billy. There was a European here before, wasn't there. And an Arab. You saw them."

Billy couldn't take his eyes off of Lupo. "Yes...the *Irlandes.*"

Irish. Bolan filed that away. "Billy, who do you think they are?"

"They're—"

"They're terrorists," Bolan finished. "What did they tell you? That they were going to punish the United States? For supporting the dictators and for the terror they inflicted in El Salvador during the civil war? Something like that?"

"I..."

"What did you think you were doing?"

"Transporting...*bombas,*" Castanado said.

"No, Billy. *You* were the bombs. You and your clique." Bolan waved his hand to encompass the ward of dying men. "This is smallpox, *viruela, comprende?* You, Mara Salvatrucha, you were the bombs. You were the carriers."

Castanado looked horrified.

"How was the fiesta, Billy? There was a party before you were to take your loads across the border. But you missed it, didn't you? You were running an errand in town. That's why you didn't get infected. All your friends did, and you would have been infected minutes after jumping in the trucks with them. It would have been a day, maybe two or three before you started showing signs of the sickness. By then some of you would be in California, others on the East Coast. Everyone you touched you would infect. Which means your people, your barrios, would be the first place the disease spread from. You hug your mother? She has it. She cooks for the *familia?* They have it. She goes to the market? Handles some fruit? Everyone on the block has it, and it spreads outside your community, and it spreads and spreads and it doesn't stop spreading. We're talking millions of people dying, Billy, and your people are the vector. How many Salvadorans have been vaccinated against smallpox?"

Bolan paused, but they both knew the answer.

"What they planned here is a crime against all humanity, against your people, the Salvadorans in the United States." Bolan's voice was as cold as the grave as he pointed at Lupo Montego. "It's genocide, and you were going to be a part of it."

"No..." The teen fell to his knees with a moan. "That's crazy. They'd kill everybody. They—"

"They're terrorists, Billy. Fanatics, and they don't care." Bolan dropped the hammer. "And they couldn't have done this without help from the top."

Castanado blinked. "What—"

"I mean your own leaders did this to you."

"No! That's impossible, they're—"

"Who's at the top, Billy? Think about it! Forty-, fifty-year-old men? They're not street gangsters living in the barrios, anymore. They're businessmen. They live in mansions, and they spit on street soldiers like you."

"But why? Why would they do it?"

"For millions and millions of dollars, and control. They and their families will be on an island someplace sipping champagne while they wait for the disease to burn itself out. With half the population or more dead, they probably think they'll own El Salvador, if not all of Central America, when it's all over. And you and Lupo?" Bolan gestured at the dying men in the isolation ward once more. "Your families are expendable. To the Irishman and the Arab, Mara Salvatrucha is expendable. Your entire race is expendable."

The young man's eyes hardened back into gangster mode. Anger kindled behind them. Bolan stepped forward, and the teen flinched.

"That's my best friend in the other room, and when I heard there was a survivor from the ranch who wasn't infected, my first instinct was to shove you into that tent with Lupo and let you bubble up and die with your amigos. But I'm going to give you a shot at redemption, Billy. And if you don't care about redemption, then you get a shot at revenge. Take your pick. I don't care. You in or out?"

The young man met the Executioner's eyes with difficulty. "What are you going to do?" he asked.

"I'm going to El Salvador. I'm betting the Arab and the Irishman have a lab down there and more of the virus, or at least the capacity to make more. I'm going to destroy it."

"And what if I say I'm out?"

"Then go," Bolan said quietly.

Billy blinked in surprise. "Go?"

"The doctors have cleared you. If you aren't in, and absolutely willing, then go take your chances with the rest of the planet." Bolan checked his watch. "I'm on a plane."

Billy C looked the Executioner squarely in the eye. "I'm in."

11

San Salvador

It was the wet season in Central America, and the daily downpour smashed down. Inside Comolapa International Airport, Bolan and Castanado stood in adjoining men's-room stalls strapping on the weapons the CIA had smuggled onto the flight for them.

Bolan checked the loads in the 93-R and tucked it away. "You ready?"

"Yeah, ready."

They headed for the car rental office. The vast majority of roads in El Salvador were unpaved, and Bolan needed a vehicle with some bite. The Executioner wore a black leather jacket with a few well-concealed extra pockets over a black shirt and matching pants. Castanado wore a blue-and-white tracksuit and stared about, wide-eyed, at the country he'd fled as a child. There wasn't much to see. The rain sheeted down, obscuring the normally mist-shrouded hills and extinct volcanoes outside the capital.

Bolan was not surprised to find a welcoming committee in the rental office.

Four men lounged about the tiny lobby like they owned it. The air around them reeked of wet wool, cigarette smoke and cheap cologne. The woman behind the rental desk pressed herself against the wall as one of the grinning men leaned over the counter whispering unpleasant endearments. Her terror was palpable. The tropical weight suits the men wore did little to conceal the bulge of firearms in shoulder holsters. They all smoked cigarettes, and all wore sunglasses despite the evening hour and the rain.

They couldn't have been more obvious if they'd had the words "Death Squad" tattooed on their foreheads, Bolan thought. Two men sat pretending to do nothing in a van parked on the curb. It wasn't Mara Salvatrucha waiting for them. It was La Sombra Negra.

The Black Shadow.

"Don't do anything unless I do," Bolan said.

The young recruit swallowed nervously, his hand moving towards his gun. "Right."

"Keep your hands off the gun. These guys will draw if they see it. Be cool. We don't want a gunfight, yet."

"Right." The young man kept his hands at his sides with an effort.

Bolan pushed open the door and the man chatting up the car rental woman turned. He looked at the man in black casually.

"*Hola*, Señor—" he gave a shrug "—Cooper?"

Bolan had expected a welcoming committee, perhaps at the hotel. The CIA's Salvadoran contacts had let slip his arrival. Bolan kept his eye on the man sitting down. He smoked a cigarette impassively and appeared to be ignoring what was going on. He was the man in command, not the talker. "That's right," Bolan said.

The talker's mirrored sunglasses came to rest on Billy. "And this would be—"

"My partner." Bolan's blue eyes burned. "We're a team."

"Really?" The man pushed himself away from the counter. "I think maybe you fucking hombres should come with us." He turned a sadistic smile on the car-rental woman. "I think maybe you'll come with me later."

The woman shuddered.

Bolan could see the way this was going. The Black Shadow didn't know what was going on. Only that the U.S. was doing something on its turf. They didn't know what it was but they intended to, and if it was profitable they probably wanted a piece of it. They wanted Bolan and Castanado, hooded, handcuffed and probably given a good opening round beating before they were driven someplace up in the hills for their official interview. Once there, torture would probably be on the table. They were establishing dominance. This initial meet and greet was the equivalent of a playground shoving match except that it could turn lethal in an instant, and the man sitting in the chair wasn't going to do anything to stop it.

Bolan shrugged. "My papers are in order, all I—"

The man and two of his thugs stepped forward, tensing with imminent violence. "We don't care about your fucking papers, Mr. Cooper. Someone wants to talk to you. Someone you'd better listen to."

Bolan pumped his right fist, snapping the man's sunglasses in two and snapping the septum supporting them. The talker sat hard on the floor, clutching his face. The Executioner's open left palm slammed into the mouth of the second man, loosening his teeth and ramming his lit cigarette into the back of his throat. He fell backward, tripping over himself as he coughed up smoke and ashes.

The third man made the mistake of going for his gun rather than diving in. He'd barely gotten his fingers on the slab-sided shape of a Colt .45 pistol when Bolan's openhanded slap violently cupped over his ear. The Executioner pulled the blow, stopping short of rupturing the man's eardrum, but the thug still fell screaming to his hands and knees as if an ice pick had been shoved into his head.

Castanado joined in and began gleefully stomping the fallen men.

Bolan kept his attention on the fourth man. He was older, balding and hadn't moved from his seat. He examined his cigarette with keen interest and sighed heavily as if annoyed. He spent a moment watching Castanado put his sneakers to his men before addressing Bolan. "You know, your little friend had better cut that out, or he isn't going to get out of this country alive."

"Billy," Bolan said.

Castanado stepped back and surveyed the stomping with satisfaction.

"You say someone wants to talk to me?" Bolan asked.

The man shook his head sadly at his brutalized thugs. "Very much."

"We'll take my car. You drive. Tell the men in the van to take these fools to the hospital."

"Of course." The man stood and smoothed his coat. He was smiling, but his eyes were unreadable behind his sunglasses. "You're the man," he said.

THE LAND ROVER DROVE into the hills outside the capital. The torrential downpour lashed the cane fields, rippling them like green waves as they passed through an endless sea of sugar plantations. Their driver's name was Javier. He didn't offer any more information and Bolan didn't bother asking. He could figure things out from long experience. Javier was likely the equivalent of a death squad noncommissioned officer. He probably was or had been a sergeant in the police or military. He casually smoked and pointed out sights of interest as they drove out of the capital despite the fact that he had been disarmed, his sunglasses had been taken away and Castanado was pressing a machine pistol against his skull from the back seat. He was a cool customer, and Bolan could tell from his body language that Javier was the type whose deceptive laziness could explode into instant violence.

Javier pointed to a sudden break in the cane fields. "There."

He pulled onto a dirt road that wound up a low hill. A dilapidated building of corrugated iron sagged with the wind. A windmill with rusted blades stood creaking next to it. A pair of covered army jeeps were parked in the clearing, as was a black Mercedes-Benz M-Class SUV. Javier pulled the Land Rover to a halt beside the other vehicles.

"Here you are, amigo."

"Here." Bolan handed Javier back his .45 and his glasses.

Javier registered mild surprise and took the weapon. *"Gracias."*

Bolan removed the crenellated iron lump of an old-fashioned U.S. pineapple grenade from his pocket. Javier drew back in his seat slightly as Bolan pulled the pin. The Executioner held down the safety lever as he clamped the pin between his thumb and forefinger. He drew the pin's length between them removing any bend and the last bit of the retaining crimp. The pin was now as straight as a needle. Bolan threaded it back into the pinhole and shook the grenade slightly so that the loose pin rattled. It would take the tiniest effort to drop the pin out.

A dying man could do it.

He put his thumb through the ring and put the grenade and his left hand in his jacket pocket. Javier nodded thoughtfully.

"Let's go," Bolan said, stepping out into the rain. He knew the goon squad had called in ahead of them to let the big boss know how the initial interview had gone. The door to the warehouse was open. Bolan nodded at Javier. "After you."

Javier called into the door. "Hey! Boss! It's me."

Silence answered. He looked back at Bolan.

"I said after you."

Javier stared at the door for a moment, squared his shoulders and stepped through. Bolan walked in after him with Castanado on his six. Half a squad of Salvadoran soldiers in olive drab and armed with M-16s faced them along with half a dozen more of the cheap-suits-and-sunglasses boys armed with big G-3 battle rifles.

Bolan kept his eyes on the royalty. A big man in an expensive suit sat at a folding table on a metal chair. It was gloomy in the cavernous warehouse interior, but his eyes seemed set in a permanent, sleepy squint. His brown hair and pale skin betrayed his European ancestry. A short beard and mustache framed his square jaw. He stared at Bolan, sizing him up like a horse trader presented with a breed he didn't recognize.

A beautiful woman sat next to him. She wore a simple, white cotton Salvadoran peasant's dress. Her long black hair fell down to her hips. Her huge dark eyes stared at Bolan with a spark of recognition he didn't like.

Javier gestured toward the man at the table. "It is my pleasure to introduce you to Colonel Escottoriano Clellando."

The colonel jerked his head at Bolan. "Search him."

Two men with rifles started forward.

"Boss, I wouldn't do that," Javier said.

The colonel smiled. "You wouldn't, Javier?"

"No, Boss." Javier stared at Bolan's left hand where it sat in his pocket cradling the grenade. "I would not."

A look passed between Javier and the colonel, and the colonel waved the two men away.

Bolan knew his machine pistol and even the prepped grenade were probably excusable. But the camera hidden in his belt buckle would probably be regarded as a major faux pas.

Bolan looked in the corner behind the colonel and his woman. An old rusted-out zinc bathtub lay on a plastic tarp. A plastic shower curtain hung open on a hoop of curtain rod above it. The tub was stained with more than rust, and brown streaks old and new streaked the cracked plastic curtain. A chain saw and a can of gas lay on the tarp by the tub.

Bolan smiled. "That for me?"

Clellando laid thick fingers on his chest in mock offense. "Oh, no, no, no. Not for you." An ugly smile split the big man's face as he pointed a finger at Castanado. "But you know, these Mara Salvatrucha scumbags—this is something they understand. It stimulates... conversation."

"So what can I do for you, Colonel?" Bolan asked.

"What can I do for you?" the colonel countered.

Bolan decided it was cards on the table time. "I'm going to take down Mara Salvatrucha."

The colonel leaned back in his seat and smiled delightedly. "Really?"

"A certain branch of it, at least."

"Well, I wish you luck."

The woman lifted a chin haughtily. "I will light a candle for you."

Bolan locked eyes with the colonel. "Someone in Mara Salvatrucha is tight with al Qaeda. They attempted to launch a terrorist attack against the United States and failed. I followed them here."

Bolan knew he'd hit paydirt as Clellando's face went flat. The woman went pale. The colonel rose. He was big, six foot four, and running 250 pounds. Behind the drowsy mastiff exterior, his eyes were as hard as flint. "Perhaps you and I should take a walk."

The woman rose. "Perhaps I should—"

"Stay here," Clellando said. The colonel strode across the warehouse and out into the downpour.

Bolan spoke out of the corner of his mouth to Castanado. "Stay here. Don't do anything, but don't let anyone mess with you."

The young man was clearly uncomfortable being babysat by the Black Shadow.

"You're MS, one hundred percent." Bolan shrugged. "Have a seat, clean your fingernails with your knife."

Billy took a seat on a crate as Bolan turned away. The sound of the Mikov knife Bolan had given him echoed as Bolan walked outside.

The colonel stood squinting up into the rain. He smiled at Bolan and spoke conversationally. "Tell me why I should not have my man on the roof shoot you and then listen to your little scumbag friend scream while I cut him into kindling?"

Bolan took the grenade out of his pocket and turned his hand over. The safety pin slid out and fell to the mud. "How's that?"

The colonel watched the rain spatter on the ugly iron lump in Bolan's hand. "Okay, so why should I help you?"

"It's in your best interest. I'm going to take out an enemy of yours," Bolan said.

"So what do you want?"

"For now? I'll settle for a name."

Clellando spent several moments staring at Bolan. "Franco. Jess Franco."

Bolan nodded. "I owe you." He reached behind his back and drew a tagged Glock. "A gift, from my government."

Clellando took the machine pistol with the delighted eye of an aficionado and flicked the selector lever. "Full-auto?"

"And laser sight," Bolan confirmed. "CIA special."

Clellando happily played the laser against the wall of the warehouse. "And how will I contact you?"

"I don't think you'll have any problem finding me, and I won't have any problem finding you."

The colonel snorted and tucked the pistol away.

"Billy!" Bolan called. "We're out of here."

Castanado trotted out grinning and folding his switchblade shut.

Clellando spoke as Bolan began to turn away. "That old grenade. It's a dud, yes?"

Bolan held out his right hand. "Nice doing business with you, Colonel."

Clellando grinned, knowing he was right and stuck out his hand to shake. "I knew it."

The colonel's grin disappeared as Bolan palmed the grenade into his hand like a magic trick. "Did you? Did you really?"

Clellando's fingers instinctively white-knuckled down on the safety lever as Bolan turned away and climbed into the Land Rover. The Colonel snarled at Javier to come fish the pin out of the mud as the Executioner drove away.

San Salvador

"Your colonel's a bad, bad boy, Mack."

Bolan sat in the CIA safehouse and stared into his laptop as Kurtzman spoke to him over a real-time video link. He had downloaded the video from the belt camera and sent it north. Kurtzman wasn't telling him anything he didn't already know. Colonel Escottoriano Clellando hadn't risen to the top of his death squad by selling magazine subscriptions.

"He rose to the rank of captain during the civil war in the 1980s. During that time he attended the U.S. Jungle Warfare Training Center in Panama and then went through the Ranger school at Fort Benning. His psychological evaluation showed some disturbing anomalies."

Bolan knew El Salvador had been one of the final battlegrounds of the cold war. The United States had staunchly supported the government. The Communists had funneled in vast amounts of aid to the rebels through Cuba and Nicaragua. In a bloody, decade-long civil war of rain forest fighting and village burning, a man with Colonel Clellando's skills wouldn't be washed out of the program for any "psychological anomalies."

They would be put to good use.

"So he returned to El Salvador and was promoted to major. He raised and trained several cadres of Special Forces units. However, according to U.S. military observers on the ground, they acted more like shock troops," Kurtzman said.

Bolan didn't have to see the reports. Clellando's men would have specialized in assassinations, kidnappings and atrocities in disputed areas. Their job would have been to keep the local population down and nonrevolutionary. Terror would have been their number-one tool. They had been given U.S. Army Ranger training and used it like Nazi storm troopers.

Kurtzman continued. "Right before the war ended he was promoted to colonel. With the official end of hostilities, he drops off the radar. The CIA isn't exactly sure how he got involved with La Sombra Negra."

Bolan was sure. For a man like Clellando, it would have been the only real career track left for him in peacetime. With a democratic government, a man of his reputation would never reach the rank of general. His wartime atrocities would similarly prevent his running for office, and Clellando was a man who wanted wealth and power. Despite peace, the right-wing fringe of the government and the military would have uses for such a man and such an organization. As his power grew, the line between right-wing government enforcer and crime lord increasingly blurred. The Black Shadow didn't hate Mara Salvatrucha because of any leftist leanings or because they had started out as ex-rebels in the civil war. That was just window-dressing for public relations and preaching to the faithful.

La Sombra Negra hated MS-13 because they were their competitors in crime.

"What about the woman?" Bolan asked.

"The local CIA branch considers her a woman of extreme interest."

Bolan considered the gaunt, almost cruel sensuality she'd exuded. "What's so interesting about her?"

"She's reputed to be the mistress of one of the most powerful gang leaders in the capital."

Bolan nodded. "Jess Franco."

"How'd you know?" Kurtzman asked.

"What's the lowdown on her?"

"Soledad Miranda Korda. Until two years ago she was the highest priced escort in San Salvador. Generals, politicians, visiting dignitaries of note, all sought her favor."

"And now she's attending clandestine meets with the head of La Sombra Negra."

Kurtzman raised a knowing eyebrow. "So she's a double agent."

"Yeah, but for who?"

Kurtzman considered the problem. "Colonel Clellando is brutal and callous enough to send his woman into his enemy's arms. I'd say Franco is subtle enough to do the same."

"And Korda's a kept woman playing games with two of the most dangerous men in El Salvador."

"You think she's playing both sides against the middle?"

"Get me more on her, Bear. Rumors, hearsay, anything. I'll need an address, as well."

Castanado came trotting into the room breathlessly. "Matt!"

"What have you got, amigo?"

"I went back to my old barrio."

"And? I threw them the sign." He held up his hands in the *M* formation. "They didn't throw it back, man."

"They follow you?" Bolan asked.

He nodded. "I'm almost sure of it."

"How many?"

"Two, I think. I looked out the window of the lobby. They're watching from across the street."

Bolan reached into his kit and pulled out a com link and a pair of binoculars. "Go up on the roof. I'm going out the back. Point them out to me."

The young man took the binoculars and the radio. "You aren't going to kill them, are you?"

Bolan measured the doubt in the young man's eyes.

He still felt loyalty to his old clique. "I'm not after the boys from the barrio, Billy. I'm after the big dogs, the traitors at the top."

Castanado nodded. He took the gear and followed as Bolan strode to the stairs. The teen went up, and Bolan went down to the street. He took the back door through the hotel kitchen and headed south two blocks. He turned right for two blocks and then began winding his way back, circling to bring himself across the street from his hotel and behind their tail. Two young men in blue-and-white tracksuits were doing a very poor job of looking inconspicuous. One was tall and fat, and one was small and painfully skinny. Both had cell phones. They stood at the corner of a food stand. The two gangsters drank sodas and shoveled food into their mouths while they watched the hotel. One was talking on the phone.

Bolan pressed his throat mike for confirmation. "You have me in sight?"

"Yes," Castanado said.

"These two jokers in front of me them?"

"That's them."

The Executioner walked up to his targets and cracked their skulls together hard. They dropped to the pavement, dazed.

Bolan turned. People on the street, sensing danger, scattered. Bolan took the still-open cell phone. Someone was demanding to know what was happening. The

Executioner spoke slowly in English. "You tell that piece of shit Billy C that I'm coming. You tell him I didn't track him all the way from Mexico for fun. I'm going to kill him." Bolan snapped the phone shut and was gone before the gang members knew what had hit them.

"Billy, you get all that?" Bolan said once he'd cleared the scene.

"Yeah, I got it."

"Good, get out of there. Take your gun, your knife and fifty bucks. There's an envelope in my kit bag. Take it and memorize it. That's your cover story. Find a place to hide. Tomorrow morning make some calls. Put out the word that an American is hunting you and you want to come in."

There was silence on the link.

"Billy, I need you to do this. Your cover will be believable, and the *jefes* will still be wondering what happened in Mexico. They want answers. They'll take you in."

Bolan thought Castanado was going to cut the link. "I trust you, Matt, but I can't wear a wire. They'll kill me."

"You don't have to." Bolan decided to display some trust. "You know that pistol I gave you—Lupo's?"

"Yeah."

"There's a tracer in it. Inside the laser sight. When they call you back and tell you they're bringing you in, you call me and tell me we're a go. I'll be tracking you. Even when I can't see you, I'll know exactly where you are."

Another long silence followed.

"Remember Lupo. Remember your homies back in Mexico and how they died," Bolan said.

"For revenge. I will do it," Castanado replied.

SOLEDAD KORDA LEANED on the rail of her penthouse balcony and looked down on the city of San Salvador. Any hint of the cooling evening downpour had disappeared, save for a still humidity thick enough to cut with a machete.

Korda had been born into the lowest levels of squalor, but now she resided in luxury.

"You've done well for yourself," the Executioner spoke from behind her.

Bolan had to give the woman credit. She didn't jump or cry out. Her shoulders tensed almost imperceptibly, then she languidly turned, leaning against the rail as she regarded him. She eyed the machine pistol in Bolan's hand. "Do you really think you need that?"

"There's a box of ammo and a spare clip for a .25 pistol in your nightstand drawer," Bolan said. The black tube of his sound suppressor never wavered from where it pointed between her perfectly sculpted eyebrows. "Where's the gun?"

Korda's slightly downturned lips curled into a lascivious smile. She unbelted her black silk kimono and opened it with teasing slowness. She held it open by the lapels and cocked her head at Bolan in speculation. She wore nothing beneath her kimono but an elastic sleeve holster on her left leg. A tiny pistol was holstered high against her thigh. "Come and get it," she said.

Bolan ignored the double-edged suggestion. "Two fingers, draw it slow and throw it here."

The woman sighed and drew the weapon with her thumb and forefinger and tossed it to the tiles. The pistol spun to a stop at Bolan's feet. He kicked it beneath a chaise lounge.

Korda shrugged and just the movement of her collarbones was worth the price of admission. "I am defenseless."

"You're playing a very dangerous game," Bolan said.

Korda slowly reached for a flute of champagne. Her eyes roved up and down Bolan's body over the rim of the glass as she took a long swallow. "You won't hurt me."

"No, but Franco will carve you like a turkey, and Clellando will truss you like a pig and saw you up in a zinc tub when they discover you're working them both."

Again there was a tiny tense of the shoulders, and again she relaxed smiling against the railing. "Do you know what every whore wants?"

Bolan did. "A stranger, handsome and kind, to come and take them out of the life and make them an honest woman before they become too old, too scarred, and too drug addicted to do anything except die diseased in a gutter."

"Very good." Korda's features turned harsh and mocking as she jerked her chin at the city below. "So if you happen to see Prince fucking Charming in San Salvador, you give him my business card. Until then, you want to hurt me? Do it. You want to fuck me? Do it." She held up a tapered forefinger and then dropped it and dangled it impotently. "You don't have the *cojones?* Leave the way you came. You're boring me."

Bolan crossed the patio in three strides. Korda's jaw tightened as he grabbed her shoulders, but it was from the pain of his grip rather than any fear. She lifted her chin up to him, waiting for the blow. Bolan stared into her dark eyes and read them like a book. There was no challenge in her eyes. She wouldn't resist him. She was a woman who had learned to endure what she could not forgive.

Bolan relaxed his grip slightly, but he held her gaze with his own. "Whose side are you on?" he asked.

She was reading him as well, and she stared up into Bolan's blue eyes for several long moments. "What if I said my side?"

"What if I said I was on your side?"

Her smile turned predatory, but something else moved behind her eyes. Perhaps hope, or desperation, but both were things she had long ago learned to conceal from herself as much as others. She leaned into Bolan and took a deep breath.

"You want a name," she said after a long pause.

"I want the Irishman and the Arab."

Korda looked at Bolan with doomed eyes. "The Arab is a Saudi, and his name is Salah Samman."

Bolan knew the name and the atrocities associated with it. The man was a wanted terrorist and the slaughter of innocents was his game. "And the Irishman?"

"The call him 'The Professor,' but his name is Drayton."

The name meant nothing to Bolan, but he was sure Aaron Kurtzman could do something with it. The Executioner released his grip on the woman. "I have to go."

She looked up at him. Hope moved behind her gaze. "And what of me?"

"You want out. I can make that happen. A new country, a new name, a new face," Bolan said gently.

Korda's lips trembled. "Do you know why I am a whore?"

There was never a good reason, but Bolan could tell she wanted to talk.

"My father borrowed money to start a business. He borrowed money from the wrong people. The business failed, but the interest on the debts grew. They grew insurmountable. I was attending university. I was the pride of the family. So at his creditor's suggestion, he was going to sell my little sister."

It was an old and ugly story and one achingly familiar to the Executioner. It was just such a situation that had started his War Everlasting. Except Soledad Korda was not a soldier. She could not take up the gun against her enemies. She had fought back with the only weapon she had. "So you took her place."

"I became the hardest working whore in San Salvador, and I was by far the smartest. I stayed out of the gutter and away from the pimps. I searched for the men with the money. The war was on, so I sought out the rebel leaders who financed their operations with drug money, the army officers who lined their pockets from looting and pillaging, the judges and police officers who could call off the death squads if they were bribed enough and the American CIA men and military observers who had fluid expense accounts. I learned to seek out the deepest, ugliest desires of such men, and to give it to them so they came back begging for more. I paid off my father's debts. I put my sister through medical school." She stared up at Bolan, daring him to despise her. "And there is nothing you can imagine that I have not done."

"You're afraid they'll go after your family."

"I do not talk to my father. My mother will not talk to me. My sister is grateful, but she moved to Costa Rica. She is a pediatrician with a practice of her own and respect in the community. She loves me, but I am a whore, and an embarrassment. Nevertheless, when my betrayal becomes known, Mara Salvatrucha and al Qaeda will go after my family."

"My government can protect your family."

"No, they can't, and I do not want my family protected. I do not want them to know. What I want is Franco, Drayton and Samman dead. I want you to kill him and his friends. I want you to kill them all. I want you to burn them to the ground and then put them under it." Korda's eyes were steel as she stared up at the Executioner. "That is my price."

13

"La Sombra Negra?" Special Agent Cervantes was appalled. She took a sip from her sweating bottle of beer. They were in a hotel bar facing the beach ten minutes outside the capital. "I can't believe you got in bed with the Black Shadow."

"You look great," Bolan said.

Cervantes looked spectacular, but she wasn't being deflected. "You didn't answer my question."

"You didn't exactly ask one. You just expressed overall disapproval."

Cervantes scowled. "So, where's your little buddy?"

"Billy C? He's about a mile from here, waiting for Mara Salvatrucha to drop a dime on him."

"You let him go? Just like that?"

"I'm inserting him, with a cover."

"I've read his file. I'm not sure I'd bet my life on your little convert to the cause," Cervantes said.

"I've read your file. Prelaw enforcement," Bolan said. "You're as much a convert to the cause as he is."

"You're an infuriating man," she said, laughing.

Bolan leaned back and finished his beer. "And other than charming company, what exactly is it you're bringing to the table, again?"

Cervantes reached into her pocket and slammed down the keys to Bolan's El Camino.

"Nice." Bolan snatched up the keys. "How'd you manage it?"

"Manage, hell. I was teleconferencing with your buddy Bear while I was in quarantine and suggested half-jokingly that you might want the car. He says 'I'm on it,' and the next thing you know it's being loaded on a C-130. It got here before I did. So what's the plan?"

"Well, I have a triple agent working both La Sombra Negra and Mara Salvatrucha, and like I said I'm inserting Billy undercover."

"He's not wearing a wire, is he?"

"No, I gave him a Glock."

"Not bad," Cervantes said. "So you're going to wait until you have two or more signals in the same room."

"And then we drop the hammer on them," Bolan agreed.

"Who's the triple agent?"

Bolan slid over Soledad Korda's file. Cervantes looked at Korda's photo. "She'd be good in made for cable horror movies."

"Her life has been a horror movie, and she's an intelligence asset. Tread easy, at least until it's time not to," Bolan said.

"I hear you. So she's in bed with Franco and the Black Shadow?"

"Franco—" Bolan pushed over Clellando's file "—and him."

"Jeez, he's a real sweetheart." Cervantes shook her head as she scanned the colonel's file.

Bolan took out his phone as it buzzed against his leg. "How you doing, Billy?"

"I got the call. They're picking me up tonight," Castanado said.

"Who's coming?"

"A guy named Soni. I don't know him."

Bolan did. Kurtzman had sent him CIA files on most of Franco's inner circle, including Soni Delgado. He was a grinning psychopath. He wasn't typically an errand boy. However, things had not been going to plan for Mara Salvatrucha in the United States or Mexico.

Bolan weighed the possibilities. Castanado's cover wasn't ironclad. It was woven with some truth. He hadn't been at the hacienda for the fiesta or the attack. Witnesses in Nuevo Laredo would be able to verify it. Fleeing back to El Salvador made sense after all the disasters in the States, and it was public knowledge that Bolan was hunting him. There was a chance Mara Salvatrucha would take Billy back into the fold, if for no other reason than to use him as bait.

The flip side was that Franco had proved he was willing to kill half the population of the planet, and he had al Qaeda breathing down his neck.

Bolan knew Castanado was in for some hard questioning. Images of Tuco's corpse came to Bolan's mind. "You still down for this?" he asked.

"I'm down with it," the young man replied.

"Then take the meet. Put the knife in your sock. I'm going to send you a second gun. We'll be right behind you. Keep the faith."

Bolan hung up and turned to Cervantes.

"Tonight we roll."

BOLAN STOOD WITH Cervantes in an alley, and the few passersby saw only a couple leaning into each other in the shadows. Bolan leaned in close to peer across the street at the apartment where Castanado was waiting.

"A car is coming," Bolan said, shifting so that his face was hidden and Cervantes could do the observing. Bolan looked at his watch and detected two of the tagged Glocks. The signal strength in the tracers was getting weaker.

Cervantes peered over his shoulder. "It's two cars, a Mercedes and a BMW. Soni's getting out of the Mercedes with a couple of muscleheads, and—Jesus!"

Bolan kept his head down. "What?"

"Ali Nur-Hadj. What the hell is he doing here? Last I heard he was into bombs, not people."

Bolan grimaced. "This isn't looking good for Billy," he said.

"You want to take down these assholes now?"

Bolan took in the scene through the veil of Cervantes's hair. Delgado had three men with him. Nur-Hadj had two bodyguards. The Saudi had another briefcase with him.

Delgado shouted at the apartment. "Billy!" They weren't going in. They kept their hands under their coats near their weapons. The guards scanned the streets. They smelled a trap. "Billy!"

"We take them now." Bolan drew his pistols. "Try to take Ali alive," he said.

Castanado appeared on the apartment steps, and for a moment he held everyone's attention.

Bolan began to move. Cervantes took a flanking position behind a parked car. The Executioner went straight in with his machine pistol and Desert Eagle filling his hands.

Most of the men were MS thugs, but Ali Nur-Hadj was a wanted terrorist and his men were probably trained bodyguards. They were the primary threat. The closest one caught Bolan's motion in the corner of his eye and spun. A Russian PP-2000 was snapped free from its shoulder rig and sprayed.

The Desert Eagle boomed once in Bolan's right hand, and the gunman went down. The second guard shoved the Saudi behind the car as he drew his weapon.

Bullets whined past Bolan's head as he pointed his Beretta. Cervantes started shooting, and the bodyguard staggered as he took the hits center body mass. He snarled and aimed his submachine gun at the FBI agent. The bodyguard was wearing body armor. Bolan snapped off a burst from his Beretta that blasted the bodyguard's face apart.

Castanado stood on the steps with his Glock held out in both hands. Ali Nur-Hadj rose from behind the car with his briefcase in his hands. He started flipping dials on the lock. The young man's laser sight burned ruby bright as he leveled it at Nur-Hadj.

"Billy! No!" Bolan roared.

The Glock machine pistol snarled off a burst. The Saudi Ali screamed as his case fell from the shredded remnants of his right hand. Delgado took cover behind the Mercedes as his thugs began blasting with their handguns in all directions. Cervantes shot one down and tracked for another. Castanado shot one then yelped as his leg was kicked out from under him.

The BMW's driver threw the car into reverse, and it shot backward on shrieking tires. Bolan touched off three quick bursts through the driver's window. The glass collapsed inward, and the driver slumped against the wheel. The car crunched into a parked car and stopped.

Bolan exchanged fire with the remaining muscle. The Beretta's burst trip-hammered him backward, and the Desert Eagle slapped him down dead. Bolan whirled as the Mercedes shot forward. The Saudi was up and running, his case clutched under his arm, and he was screaming at the Mercedes driver in Arabic. The car screeched to a halt, and the driver snaked out his arm and blindly blasted backward with a submachine gun as he waited for Nur-Hadj. Bolan's Desert Eagle boomed once and the driver screamed as the .44 Magnum round took off his gun hand at the elbow.

The driver stomped on the gas, leaving the Saudi behind. Bolan methodically emptied his pistols into the car, but the driver crouched down and the sedan fishtailed off into the night. Bolan ripped free fresh magazines for his weapons. Nur-Hadj was still screaming and sprinting after the car.

"I got him!" Cervantes shouted. She held her weapon in both hands and took careful aim. "Ali! Stop or I'll shoot!"

The Saudi spun, raising a snub-nosed .38 as Cervantes fired off a double-tap. The briefcase slipped from its precarious position beneath his injured arm and dropped. Cervantes's first shot winged him in the thigh exactly as intended, but in the split second as her pistol rolled with the recoil and she touched off her second shot, the case fell like a curtain between the 10 mm hollowpoint and its human objective. Ali Nur-Hadj disappeared in a ball of orange fire.

The blast knocked Bolan to the street. He rolled

backward with the superheated concussion and came up in combat crouch with ears ringing and lights pulsing behind his eyes. The explosion had knocked down Cervantes, and she yawned her jaws wide and blinked against the blast effect.

"Matt!" Castanado shouted from the steps. "Look out!"

Soni Delgado came out of nowhere. His gun was gone. So were his eyebrows. His face was black and his hair was on fire. He held a twelve-inch meat cleaver on high. He hacked the butcher's tool down at the Executioner's face like a hatchet. Bolan crossed his empty pistols up in a defensive cross and steel grated on steel. Bolan rolled backward with the blow and rammed his heel beneath Delgado's kneecap. Cartilage crunched and Delgado staggered. The Executioner rolled to the side, dropping his spent pistols, and pulled his recon Tanto knife from its sheath.

Bolan thrust his blade up beneath Delgado's chin. The gangster shuddered and fell to the street.

Bolan wiped and sheathed his blade. He scooped up his pistols and reloaded as he jogged over to Castanado. The young man was sitting on the stoop cradling his right leg. His track pants were dark red from the calf down, and his sneaker was filling with blood. He looked up with a pained shrug. "They got me."

"Yeah." Bolan knelt and pulled a field dressing out of his jacket's inner pocket.

"I got one." Billy brightened. "And a piece of that Ali asshole."

"I know. Nice shooting, Tex," Bolan said.

Castanado beamed as Bolan wound the dressing around his leg. A bullet had gone through one side of his calf and out the other. The good news was that the bad guys were using armor-piercing ammo, so the bullet had winged through without expanding and blowing the muscle apart. It was a clean wound that had already collapsed in on itself. He'd walk with a limp for a while, but he would walk.

Bolan glanced back at Cervantes. She was up but still shaking her head. The barrio was starting to come alive with the sounds of dogs barking, chickens crowing and people shouting and screaming. Bolan quickly scanned the scene. Nur-Hadj and Delgado were dead.

Things hadn't gone exactly to plan.

Bolan pulled Castanado up and put his arm over his shoulder. "We gotta get out of here."

"Dead!" Jess Franco was pacing the pink Italian marble floor of his penthouse suite. "I want the American dead!"

Soledad Korda brought Franco a fresh gin and tonic. "So kill him," she said with a shrug.

Franco scowled and accepted the drink. He couldn't quite tell if she was being sarcastic or simply thought he had that kind of power. Things were going from bad to worse. Ali Nur-Hadj had liked playing with explosives just a little too much in Franco's opinion, and now they were scraping him off the sidewalk like gum. Franco could have predicted that, but Soni Delgado was dead, and that left Franco deeply disturbed.

He turned to the woman. "So how are things with soldier boy?"

Korda peered at the bubbles in her flute of champagne. "Which one?" She arched a bemused eyebrow.

Franco grinned. She was the one woman he had never grown tired of. The first time he'd laid eyes on her he had to have her. The fact that she was willing to sleep with his enemies to learn their secrets turned him on even more. "Let's start with Clellando."

"The colonel has met with the American. They plot against you."

Salah Samman ceased his languorous smoking and gazing at the volcano. "La Sombra Negra. They are a real threat?" he asked.

Franco spit. "Babykillers. Kidnappers. Assassins. But, yes, they are a danger. The death squads and the United States had the same aims during the civil war. It is not good that this American prick went and took a meeting with them."

"So it is war?"

"War?" Franco scowled. "The death squads are aligned with the right-wing faction of the government. They have the tacit approval of much of the military and police. If we go to war, they will call it a war against organized crime and use it as an excuse to try to wipe us out."

Samman considered the situation. "Perhaps we should step up our timetable."

The professor strode into the room, grinning. "Perhaps we should just kill the bloody son of a bitch as Miss Korda suggested, and this sodding Colonel Clellando with him."

"Oh, and how are we supposed to do that, Professor?" Franco felt his blood begin to boil again. "Use the fucking scientific method?"

The Irishman flashed a smile. "No, simple mathematics."

Franco's scowl returned. This Irishman seemed to treat every situation like some kind of game. It was a game they were currently losing. "What are you talking about?"

"Simple. We've had problems in D.C., Los Angeles, Mexico and now here in El Salvador. They all have a common denominator."

"Yeah, Chico, you're right. And the common denominator is the American!"

The Irishman nodded. "You're half right."

Franco's face went blank. "Half?"

The professor cast a glance at Samman and Korda and then began whispering in Franco's ear.

The most dangerous man in El Salvador smiled like a kid on Christmas Day at what he heard.

"The Glocks. They're moving," Aaron Kurtzman said over the secured satellite connection.

"How many?" Bolan asked.

"Thirty. They're converging on a warehouse a few miles west of your position. Something's up."

Bolan glanced at his watch and activated the tracker. The indicators showed that the signal strength was failing.

"Gadgets says we have only a few hours of signal left," Kurtzman said.

It would be their last opportunity to act while they had the advantage of the tracers. "We're moving," the Executioner said.

"Thirty guns, Striker. Just what are you expecting to do?"

Bolan knew what he had to do. "I'm going to have to go someplace I didn't want go."

Kurtzman was quiet for moment. "Black Shadow."

"I don't have a lot of other options."

"You be real careful around this Clellando character. The more I learn about him the less I like it."

"Tell me the good news."

"The good news is that in his debriefing Billy reported that Lupo gave the Irishman a Glock. Based on the lot numbers and those recovered from the ranch in Nuevo Laredo, we're ninety percent sure that he's at the warehouse. So is Franco. They're up to something."

"What else?"

"We have a line on the Irishman. His name is Dr. Bruce Drayton. He got his doctorate in epidemiology at Oxford."

Bolan could see where this was going.

"He's currently supposed to be on sabbatical in Central America," Kurtzman continued. "We informed MI-6, and twelve hours ago their agents secured his house and his research lab in Oxford. His house turned up nothing, but at his lab all of his records have been removed. He was supposed to be working on a strain of flu virus, but all his samples have been destroyed. The lab is empty and was professionally sterilized before he left."

"What about his lab assistants?"

"MI-6 is trying to track them down. They no longer appear to be in England. Reading between the lines of his project reports, it seems he may have been working with the smallpox virus for over a year, right under the university staff's nose."

"So how did Drayton get hold of the virus in the first place?"

"You're going to have to ask him that," Kurtzman stated.

Bolan checked his watch. "I intend to."

"Best bet, Samman was his connection. We don't know if it was leftover weaponized virus the Russians didn't destroy or straight Variola, but regardless, we've seen the results in Mexico."

"Speaking of which, how's Carl?" Bolan asked.

"He's clearing up fine. A little spotty still, but he's up and around."

"Bear, I gotta go." Cervantes was donning her raid suit. "I'll call you when we're rolling. See if you can line me up an observation satellite," Bolan said.

"Will do. Bear, out."

Bolan clicked his phone shut. "Go wake up Billy."

Cervantes frowned. "You want to bring him in on this?"

Bolan didn't, but he needed every warm body he could get. "We'll keep him back, as insurance." Bolan scooped up his car keys. "Besides, he's been dying to drive the El Camino."

15

Bolan checked his watch. He and Cervantes had broken into a flower shop that would not be opening for another two hours. Ten of the Glock tracer signals had gone out. Bolan had the other twenty pinpointed down the street, but their signal was growing so weak that the telltales in his watch barely registered them and the NSA satellite far overhead had lost them completely.

Suddenly a single full strength signal was rapidly approaching his position. A van drove down the almost deserted early-morning street. It pulled past the flower shop and turned into the alley. A few moments later, Javier came in through the back door. His eyes widened as he took them in. Bolan and Cervantes were both wearing raid suits and body armor, and were festooned with weapons from head to foot.

"Good morning, amigo," Javier said, peering around. "Where is your little friend?"

Bolan shrugged. "Got himself shot."

"Ah, well." Javier had clearly heard about the gunfight. He ran his eye up and down Cervantes with appreciation. "I like your replacement."

The FBI agent stared at Javier like he was pond scum but bit back any reply.

"So, you say you have Jess Franco, possibly the terrorist Salah Samman and this Irish professor you were talking about?"

Bolan lifted his chin toward the street outside. "Half a block down. The auto shop." The palatial warehouse down the street was clearly a chop shop and clearing house for stolen vehicles.

Javier was obviously aware of that. "Why meet there?" he asked.

"The attempted attack out of Mexico was based on automobile transportation. They may be trying the same trick again," Bolan said.

Javier's face went hard. "You are going to have to give us something more than 'The attempted attack out of Mexico was based on automobile transportation.'"

"What if I said information is on a need-to-know basis?"

"I would say, with respect of course, that this is not your country. This is more than just turf war with Mara Salvatrucha. We are now talking about enemies of the state. La Sombra Negra defends the state. Indeed, we are the state. We hold the line. You want to keep secrets?" Javier's hands dropped down to his sides like a gunfighter. "Maybe you and your new friend don't leave this flower shop alive. Regardless of what you might have in your pocket."

Bolan locked his gaze with Javier, and the Salvadoran wasn't blinking. He knew the man wasn't posturing. He believed what he was saying.

Bolan threw his cards on the table. "Smallpox."

Cervantes sucked in a breath. She clearly didn't approve of the disclosure.

Javier stared for a moment, still holding his poker face. *"Viruela?"*

"Weaponized by the Irishman," Bolan confirmed. "We believe it was smuggled out of Russia by Samman with al Qaeda money. They were going to release it across the U.S. border from Mexico. They were using their own people, infecting them without their knowing it. They would have dispersed across the U.S. while the virus incubated inside their bodies. By the time they started showing symptoms, they would have infected thousands. It would have spread like wildfire across the United States and very likely the world. We got lucky and contained the situation in Mexico, but we have every reason to believe they have more of the virus in stock somewhere here in Central America."

Javier had no immediate reply.

Bolan changed the subject. "How many men did you bring?"

"Two squads. One in the van and another is hanging back. All trusted men, with rifles."

Bolan made a decision. "Bring them forward."

"You have a plan?" Javier asked.

"I was going to sneak in, but if we have half a platoon, then we might as well go in full-assault. It's a cul-de-sac, so deploy four men on the back door and put it in a cross fire. The rest of us will go in the front," the Executioner said.

Javier opened his cell phone and made two calls. Soon eighteen members of his squad had packed into the flower shop and filled it with a fog of nervous cigarette smoke.

Bolan examined the men critically. Their short-barreled G-3 KA-4 assault rifles were casually slung with the stocks folded. None of them were wearing any web gear, and their few spare magazines were stuffed into their suit pockets. Most were in their twenties, far too young to be veterans of the civil war.

Bolan knew taking down Mara Salvatrucha's leader was a plum assignment. Vast amounts of territory would be taken along with the resulting wealth and status. Most of these men had been picked because of their family or political connections. They were intimidators and thugs, dilettantes in violence rather than soldiers or cops. Most of them seemed to have suddenly realized this was going to be an assault rather than an assassination or kidnapping. In their favor, they all seemed to be wearing soft body armor under their suits.

Javier caught Bolan's judging look and rolled his eyes as if to say good help was hard to find.

"They speak English?" Bolan asked.

"All of them."

The gathered men looked at Bolan.

"Buddy system." Bolan held up two fingers and twined them. "We deploy by twos. No one shoots unless Javier and I start it, or someone shoots at you first. Got it?"

The assembled men nodded, leaning closer and holding their weapons with renewed purpose.

Bolan figured there was no use trying to set out any more of a plan. If they could just stick to that much, it would be a miracle. He knew all hell would break loose once the first shot was fired.

"Buddy up! Lock and load!" Bolan pointed out the window to both sides of the street as they readied their weapons. "Alternate, by twos! Move when I move! Stop when I stop! Look to Javier! Look to me! Fear nothing!"

The Executioner hit the street with Cervantes on his six. In the flower shop, Javier directed his men by twos to cover both sides of the street. Their dress shoes clacked on the cobblestones as they deployed, but it couldn't be helped. Bolan ran to the mouth of the cul-de-sac and held up his fist as he crouched behind a pickup. The Black Shadow skidded to a stop, taking cover behind parked cars or plastering themselves against buildings.

Cervantes spoke low, echoing what Bolan was thinking. "So where are the lookouts?"

Bolan checked his watch. The tracer signals inside the chop shop hadn't moved. Nothing was moving. There was no one in sight. It was 6:15 a.m. on a Sunday in San Salvador on the industrial side of town.

Javier scuttled forward to their position cradling an Uzi. "What's happening?"

"Nothing." Bolan lifted his chin towards the cul-de-sac. The only thing missing was a lone tumbleweed blowing through and the howl of a coyote.

Javier scowled and spoke quietly into his cell phone in Spanish. "The American thinks it's a trap. I think maybe he's right." Javier's scowl deepened as he listened to the answer. Javier put his phone away. "Colonel Clellando says it doesn't matter. He orders us to take the building."

Javier flinched as he met the Executioner's eyes. They both knew Bolan wasn't taking orders from anybody. Bolan thumbed his com link. "Control, what do you have on satellite?"

"The resolution is not ideal, Striker," Barbara Price reported. "We're on the far side of the observation window. But we have no apparent heat signatures or movement on the rooftops or within a block around the target."

Bolan didn't like it. He spoke to Javier. "You're going in?"

Javier sighed. "I have my orders." He looked at Bolan hopefully.

There really wasn't any choice. "All right, let's do it."

Bolan rose and sprinted across the cul-de-sac. The men followed hot on his heels. Two huge folding doors of corrugated iron opened into the bays of the shop. Bolan went to the steel security door to the office and slapped a packaged breaching charge against the lock. "Fire in the hole!"

He stepped away and hit his detonator box. The shaped charge blasted out the lock, and the door vibrated open on its hinges. The Executioner's flash-stun grenade flew in, and a second one thrown by Cervantes followed it. Thunder rattled the shop's window and smoke and the fireflies of pyrotechnic secondary effect eddied out the door.

Bolan burst into the chop shop, the red beam of his carbine's designator blazing. Smoke and lights spun about in the crosscurrents from the grenade blasts. Bolan kicked in the back office door and entered the shop. The Black Shadow followed Bolan and Cervantes, deploying to either side along the walls at Javier's order. Bolan made his way between a matched pair of Corvettes and paused in the shadow of a silver Porsche on a hydraulic lift.

Thirty Glock 18-C machine pistols lay piled on top of a folding table. Each pistol was unloaded with the slide racked back on an empty chamber. Each pistol's laser designator-tracer unit hung out condemningly.

"We are so screwed," Cervantes said.

They'd been betrayed.

Barbara Price echoed the sentiments across the satellite link. "We have movement, Striker! Armed men coming out onto the adjoining roofs! Men deploying into the cul-de-sac! Platoon strength!"

The first light antitank rocket hissed through the skylight and eclipsed the table of machine pistols in fire. Bolan judged the rocket's flight from the smoking line of its exhaust. Men began shouting and screaming and firing their weapons in random directions while Javier roared at them to take cover. Bolan stepped out from under the Porsche and fired his grenade launcher through the shattered skylight. A second rocket hissed down from the opposite direction and smashed into a car. Glass and car parts flew through the shop's interior like shrapnel.

Automatic rifles opened up from the street, punching swarms of holes through the shop's big bay doors. Men fell as random bullets from the hailstorm hit them. A third rocket shrieked down and left a red Audi in smoldering ruin. A death squad gunner ran out the office door and was cut to pieces in the cross fire. Another stood by one of the bay doors, trying to work the buttons to raise it. A rocket fired from the street hit the door and detonated. The man screamed as the shaped-charge warhead burned through the thin iron and fried him alive. The smell of roasting human flesh joined the stench of high explosive and burning gasoline.

Javier knelt by the inner office door firing bursts into the street.

"Keys!" Bolan roared. "Get the keys!"

Javier blinked and suddenly nodded. *"Sí!"* He leaped into the office and ripped the pegboard of keys from the wall. A rocket hissed into the office after him, and the windows blew out as he dived into the shop. He skidded to a stop by Bolan. The Executioner scanned the burning shop, then snatched the keys to the two Corvettes and the Porsche from the hooks.

The shark-shaped noses of the two Corvettes were pointed at the bay doors. Bolan flicked open his phone and punched the preset. It answered halfway through the first ring. "Matt?"

"Billy! I need you now! We're in the shop!"

Bolan could hear the car roaring to life over the phone. "I'm coming!" Castanado said.

Bolan clicked off his phone and tossed Javier a set of keys. "Put it in neutral and jam down the accelerator!"

Javier had already guessed the plan.

Bolan shouted at Cervantes. "The bay doors! Get them open!"

Cervantes vaulted the charred remains of the dead man and hit the buttons to raise the doors. The two doors were already pierced like sieves and as they began to rattle upward the fusillade intensified. Bolan jammed the keys into the Corvette, and it roared into life. A line of bullets walked up the hood and spiderwebbed the passenger side of the windshield. Bolan jammed down the accelerator with a wrench and rolled out as he put the car into gear.

The Corvette's tires screamed against the slick concrete floor and then bit in and sent the car shooting out into the street. Bullets began striking it from every direction. The second car shot forward. Javier spun and fell as a bullet hit him. Bolan grabbed him and dragged him out of the line of fire. He laid him back against a rolling tool chest, then dropped the Porsche down from the lift.

"Give me the keys!"

Bolan turned to find four G-3 rifles pointed at his face. Fear and desperation sweated from the pores of the men behind them.

"I think you boys want to wait for—"

"Give me the fucking keys!"

Bolan gave the man the keys. One of them stared back at their commander reluctantly as they piled into the Porsche. "But, Javier, he's—"

"He's fucking dead!" the ringleader snarled. "We go!"

The Porsche squealed out of the shop. Some of the Black Shadow boys at the back of the shop ran forward shouting as they were abandoned.

The four men sprayed their rifles out the windows awkwardly while bullets struck the Porsche in a lethal cross fire. The Porsche fishtailed as one of its tires was shot out. A rocket hissed down in a smoking white line from the rooftop above, and the Porsche went up in a spectacular fireball that shattered windows on both sides of the street.

The El Camino came roaring through the smoke and flames. Castanado wove the black car through the burning wrecks as if he were threading a needle. Unlike the other hapless vehicles littering the cul-de-sac and the shop, the El Camino had been modified with bulletproof glass and Kevlar curtains in the body panels. Bullets cratered the black exterior but did not penetrate. Castanado yanked the parking brake and spun the vehicle into the shop bay in a textbook bootlegger's turn.

Bolan snarled at the crouching Black Shadow boys. "Get Javier in the back! Candy! Get in front with Billy!"

Javier had been shot through the shoulder and was bleeding a river. Bolan jumped into the truck bed with La Sombra Negra and jammed a field dressing into the wound. The attackers were going to rush the shop at any second. Bolan slammed his palm down on the roof of the car. "Go! Go! Go!"

The El Camino's four hundred horses roared in willing response, and it tore back into the bloody dawn. The car's open truck bed was a platform. "Shoot!" Bolan boomed. "Shoot!"

The Black Shadow gunners fired their rifles at the rooftops. Men with M-16s fired at the car from the rooftops and the street. The men who had been charging the shop suddenly found themselves in the car's way, and they threw themselves still shooting. One of the Black Shadow hardmen twisted and fell over the tailgate as a bullet took him in the face. Bolan felt a bullet strike his armor and then a second, but he grimly fired on and emptied the street of the shooters before them.

A rocket hissed and blasted into the cobblestones two yards ahead of the car. Castanado drove through the smoke and flame. The El Camino was mostly bulletproof, but a light antitank weapon would end the game in an instant. Bolan turned and fired at a man on a roof snapping a fresh rocket into the firing position. He screamed and twisted as the flying fragments tore him and his loader apart.

Bolan caught sight of the unmistakable silhouette of Colonel Clellando on the roof. The colonel was firing his Glock on full-auto at the fleeing car. Bolan raised his rifle, but a bullet took another Black Shadow man who cried out and fell against him. Bolan's burst went high and wide just as Castanado brought the El Camino into a screaming turn that nearly threw Bolan out of the back. The car shot out into the city streets and out of the line of fire.

Javier had taken another bullet and was as white as a ghost. The remaining Black Shadow soldier had taken one in the leg and the bed of the truck was covered with their blood.

Castanado rolled down his cracked and pocked window. "Where to?"

Bolan considered the question. The military, the police and Mara Salvatrucha would be looking for them. The U.S. Embassy and the airports would be watched. The streets of the capital were unsafe and they had wounded.

"Billy," he said, "take us to your village."

Castanado stepped on the gas and sped eastward out of the city. Bolan looked back at the black smoke rising up over the city behind them. Colonel Escottoriano Clellando had betrayed his own men. He'd pulled the trigger himself.

It was a pretty safe bet that the colonel had bought himself a seat at the table of the postplague new world order.

Zapatepeque Village

Bolan's six hours of sleep had done him a world of good.

He lay in a hammock in a tiny village that hung precipitously off the side of a volcano. Castanado might try to pass himself off as a big city gangster, but the fact was he was country boy through and through, and his web of relations stretched from one side of the country to the other. It was just as well. According to Kurtzman, Bolan, Javier and Castanado were wanted by the army and the police. Clellando didn't have a line on Cervantes, but her description was being circulated in conjunction with the rest of the team.

Bolan clicked open his phone. "Soledad. Where are you?"

"The airport." The triple agent spoke in a hushed whisper, "in the bathroom."

"Where are you headed?"

"We are heading to an island off the coast of Belize, but Franco is making a stop without me."

"Where?"

"I don't know. Someplace inside the border of Honduras. He is taking a small plane. Wait…"

Bolan was pleased to see a text message scroll across his phone. It was a longitude and a latitude. "Good work. When is he leaving?"

"In three hours."

"Call me when you get to Belize."

Bolan stuck his phone into the port of his satellite link. "Control."

Barbara Price answered instantly. "This is Control, Striker. What is your situation?"

"The roads are going to be watched, and I'm running out of time. I need Jack in the air ASAP to San Salvador and a helicopter positioned at the airport waiting for him. Full warloads inside, if possible. We'll be flying into Honduran airspace at these coordinates." Bolan punched in the location. "I need real-time satellite recon of the area, if possible, and if not, at least photos. There's reason to believe this may be the location of the bio lab and virus stock."

"Affirmative, Striker. Jack will be airborne ASAP. Helicopter will be in place. Will try to arrange weapons fit with CIA station. Putting Bear on satellite recon now."

"Affirmative. Thanks, Control. Striker out."

A HELICOPTER WAS LANDING in a goat enclosure. Jack Grimaldi was flying a Huey that looked like it was of Vietnam-war-era manufacture but painted a dirty civilian grayish blue. Goats scattered, bleating, and bells tinkled in all directions. The villagers hung back, lurking in the shadows of their huts. Everyone thirty and over had long ago learned to fear helicopters. The helicopter powered down, and Grimaldi popped out of the cockpit grinning from ear to ear.

The goats had lost their fear of the helicopter, and Grimaldi reached down and scratched one between the horns as it gently butted against him. His smile went up in wattage as he looked around the little village. It had been a while since he'd been in El Salvador. "Nice," he said. Cervantes ambled up from the other side of the village, and the pilot shot Bolan a look of approval. "Very nice."

Javier limped up with an arm over Billy's shoulder. The Black Shadow soldier's face was a ghastly gray. "That's the rest of your strike team?" Grimaldi asked.

"Yeah. Speaking of which, how's Carl?" Bolan said in reply.

"Pissed. He wanted to come along, but the doctors haven't cleared him yet."

Bolan sighed. Things would have looked a lot brighter with Lyons on his six.

Grimaldi nodded sympathetically. "By the way, in case you didn't know, your name is mud in El Salvador.

You got everyone and their brother looking for you. It's way beyond anything the CIA can smooth over. According to intelligence, Javier is a dead man. Officially, he's wanted in connection to terrorism. Unofficially, there's a ten-million-dollar bounty on his head."

"How are things stateside?"

"It's only a matter of time before the FBI downgrades Cervantes's 'special detached duty' to 'get your ass back here immediately.'"

It was nothing Bolan didn't already know. He was surprised it hadn't happened already.

Castanado thrust out his chin defiantly. "And me?"

"You?" Grimaldi grinned. "Franco's put out the word, and a million on your head. You're wanted, dead or alive, from Canada to Caracas."

The young man was pleased with his desperado status.

"So what's the good news?" Bolan asked.

"We have your lab."

They moved into a hut, and Grimaldi spread out a map and satellite photos on the plank table. "DEA says it used to be a drug smuggler's transfer point for weapons going across the border into El Salvador during the civil war, and now it's a Mara Salvatrucha transfer point for drugs. The Salvadoran-Honduran border in that region is in dispute, so the location is a geopolitical gray area." Grimaldi's fingertip wandered over a photo. "You have a small ranch, barbed-wire fence and a guard tower, some military-style tents, and here you have three trailers."

Bolan examined the three structures. "That's where they're brewing it up," he said.

"No doubt. They also have an airstrip and about twenty to thirty men on station."

Bolan examined the terrain. The camp was in a mountain valley at high altitude. There was very little around it in the way of trees and cover. For a raid, he'd want a platoon of Special Forces dropping high-altitude low-opening under cover of night. Unfortunately, that wasn't forthcoming, and he had about two hours before Franco showed up with an army of bodyguards. There was no time to set up an attack and almost no resources to attack with.

No time for anything except maybe a Trojan horse.

Bolan looked at Grimaldi. "How much do they have on Javier's head again?"

THE HELICOPTER SWEPT over the mountainous border country and orbited the encampment. They had briefly put down outside the border town of Sensuntepeque to do some shopping. Castanado was wearing his first suit. It was an off-the-rack blue pinstripe and mainly polyester, but with the mirrored blue sunglasses he had made the change from Mara Salvatrucha street gangster to La Sombra Negra young lion without missing a beat. Bolan and Grimaldi were similarly dressed. Cervantes would have been a lot harder to explain, so she had reluctantly hidden under a tarp. Javier didn't require any dressing up. Shot and half-dead, he was perfect the way he was.

The camp was hailing them desperately over the radio. The Spanish was flying too fast for Bolan or the pilot, so Cervantes whispered appropriate answers in Castanado's ear. The Executioner was banking on the lab being run by al Qaeda and MS. The Black Shadow had only joined the team recently, so there were going to be communication gaps, and the Black Shadow had focused on forming a net to pick up the fugitives.

Castanado was gleefully telling the camp they had Javier and that he was now a multimillionaire. He was also demanding permission to land and telling them to fuel up the chain saw because Colonel Clellando would be along directly.

Bolan nodded to Grimaldi. "Just land it."

The pilot ceased his circling, and Cervantes crawled back under her tarp. The helicopter dropped like a stone right into the middle of the camp while men armed with AK-47 rifles charged them from all directions. Bolan glanced at the guard tower and noted the machine gun being pointed in their direction. Bolan had guessed right. By the way they held their weapons and came out as a mob, the muscle in the camp were drug thugs rather than Black Shadow renegade soldiers or cops.

Grimaldi powered down the chopper, and he and Bolan jumped out of either side of the cockpit. Both of them slouched and held their weapons loosely. Javier eased himself out of the cabin, flinching as Castanado prodded him with his pistol. It was a gamble, but for the moment the young gangster was in charge. He was playing the rich punk risen by connections into the Black Shadow's echelons to the hilt. Bolan and Grimaldi looked slightly out of place, but a lot of the right-wingers in El Salvador were the descendants of Spanish and European colonists. They knew they could pass as very dangerous men in the pay of the Black Shadow until they opened their mouths.

Castanado was doing all the talking. He had no experience as an undercover agent, but he had the magic words working for him. Everyone knew Javier was worth ten million, and he'd miraculously caught him. Javier stumbled beside Castanado, his arm hanging in a sling and his suit stained with blood front and back.

The mob clustering around the chopper was MS, but they knew Clellando by reputation. When the colonel showed up, he would rev up the chain saw and there would a horror show they could brag about for years. The camp guards gazed upon Castanado and his prisoner like they were movie stars. Javier winced with real pain as the young man poked his injured shoulder again and laughed like a man who had won the lottery.

Bolan and Grimaldi were ignored until Castanado suddenly remembered the plan. He jerked his thumb at

Bolan and spoke in Spanish. "You, stay with the helicopter."

Bolan affected an attitude of extreme boredom as he sat in the open cabin door of the Huey. The others were ushered to the little house. Bolan spoke to the lump of tarp in the back of the cabin. "How you doing?"

"Sweating like a pig."

"I'm going to take a walk over to the trailers and—" Bolan stopped talking as a young man in fatigue pants and a denim jacket with cut-off sleeves walked up to the helicopter. He carried an AK-47. The young man had obviously pulled guard duty and looked intensely annoyed. He wanted to talk. Bolan threw out a few noncommittal grunts as the Central American patois began to run faster and thicker than his own Spanish could follow. The young man's eyes suddenly narrowed. The question had required more than some mumbled vowels of assent.

The conversation was over.

Bolan seized the man's lapels and yanked, slamming his skull into the cabin door frame, and the man collapsed in a heap on the chopper's skid.

Bolan looked around. Grimaldi had landed the helicopter so that it blocked the view of the guard tower. No one on the ground had noticed. Bolan hauled the unconscious man into the cabin and confiscated his rifle. "I'm going for a walk over to the trailers," he said to Cervantes. "Keep an eye on this one."

The heap of tarp threw out a fold that mostly covered the man, and Bolan tucked his feet under. He hopped out of the cabin and peered up at the guard tower. The two men at the top were watching the house. Bolan sprinted over to the trailers and put them between himself and the guards. The three trailers were connected by tented wooden causeways. Bolan mounted the metal steps up to a door. He gingerly tried the doorknob and found it locked.

Bolan drove the butt of the AK-47 down sharply and sheared off the knob.

The guts of the lock mechanism came out with a light pull, and the door opened. The trailer was mostly taken up by a command center. A desk with a computer and a radio took up a corner of the trailer. World maps on the walls were marked with red concentric circles. The three initial infection points were Miami, Dallas and Los Angeles.

Bolan knew he'd hit pay dirt.

He eased open the door to the second trailer, and chickens in elevated coops clucked at him. Several eggs lay in the hutches beneath the coops. Kurtzman had told him the easiest way to cultivate the virus was in fertile chicken embryos. Boxes and crates of chemicals and equipment lined the other wall. Bolan walked to the far door. He made out two voices on the other side speaking in English. Very carefully, Bolan tried the knob and found it locked. He drew his Beretta machine pistol out of its holster and threaded the sound suppressor onto the end of the barrel. The trailer door was not particularly strong, but efforts had been made to make it airtight.

Bolan stepped back and kicked in the door.

Professor Drayton and his assistant froze in shock over their work. Their table had test tubes, a centrifuge, microscopes and a few pieces of equipment Bolan didn't recognize. It was bathtub bioterrorism 101. Drayton's assistant was an attractive Middle Eastern woman. Her hair was pulled back from her face and she wore black framed glasses over her huge dark eyes.

"Keep your hands flat on the table. Don't move," Bolan said.

Drayton's face split into a smile. His green eyes bored into Bolan's without blinking. Bolan knew instantly that the doctor was crazed.

Drayton looked around. "Where are your friends?"

"You're going to account for every particle of virus," Bolan said.

Drayton raised his eyebrows. "Or what?"

Bolan leveled the Beretta at Drayton's face. "You've got about five seconds."

The staring contest began. Bolan had seen the psychopath in Drayton's eyes. When Drayton looked into Bolan's, he saw that he was not going to be captured or tortured. He was going to be executed. Drayton's eyes lost their twinkle as Bolan flicked the selector switch to 3-round burst and began counting. "One, two, three, four, f—"

"Sophie," Drayton interrupted. "Give him the file."

The woman slowly reached toward an open laptop. "The file is encrypted," she said.

"Bring it up and print it."

Drayton leaned back against the wall and crossed his arms. Bolan saw the diversion, but the distance was very short. The woman screamed like a banshee and lunged. She held a syringe in an ice-pick grip, and whatever was in it Bolan didn't want any part of it. The needle arced for Bolan's eyes. He had no choice but to fire. She fell to the floor. At the same time, Drayton took the opportunity to drop behind the lab table.

Bolan threw himself back as a stream of bullets ripped through the table and tore a line up the wall beside his head. He recognized the firing signature of a Glock 18C. The gun wasn't silenced. The scream and the automatic burst would have been heard throughout the camp. Bolan anticipated Drayton's next move and jumped into the air. A long burst scythed at knee level from under the table aiming for where Bolan's legs had just been. The soldier scrambled onto the table and covered its length in a stride. Drayton's eyes widened as Bolan loomed over him. He raised the Glock, but Bolan was already firing. His bursts knocked the Glock away and tore through Drayton's hands and arms. Bolan dropped down and shoved the smoking suppressor under Drayton's chin. "All of the virus, accounted for, now."

"I'll tell you something for nothing, boyo." Drayton's teeth were bloody as he smiled. "It's not all here."

Bolan could hear shouting outside. "Where?"

"Well, now, the Mara Salvatrucha lads, they proved themselves somewhat unreliable. But the Black Shadow boys, now…"

Bolan's blood went cold. Drayton saw it and smiled wider as he wheezed blood. "The colonel, Salah, and I had a meeting. We thought we might have a leak, and now we know."

Bolan knew the plan. The Black Shadow had the virus, and Colonel Clellando planned to set himself up as the emperor of Central America.

"We were going to take care of Franco when he arrived and then set a trap for you. But you got here so fast. How did you do that?"

Bolan ignored the question as he calculated. "What are you doing to Franco?"

"The device I put in his plane will have infected everyone aboard by now."

And then he would infect everyone in the camp. Bolan knew he had three sources to deal with. The virus in camp, the virus in Franco and his men and Clellando's private supply.

Drayton laughed as he read Bolan's predicament. "I figured the leak had to be Soledad, and I was right, wasn't I? I told my suspicions to the colonel. That whore? She's going to go underneath the chain saw. And the world will burn beneath what I made under my microscope."

Drayton collapsed on the floor.

Bolan rose. He opened up the minifridge in the corner of the lab and glanced at the test tubes racked within. An incubator inside a glass containment case lay next to it. Bolan took a white phosphorous grenade from his pocket and hurled it through the glass of the incubator. He closed the damaged door behind him and ran down the little tented gangway to the next trailer. He jumped over the side of the gangway and crouched beneath it as shadowy forms rushed by the vaguely translucent green plastic tenting.

Behind him the grenade detonated. The unhinged door flew open, and molten metal streaked out on streamers of smoke. The tenting blackened, wrinkled and burned.

The Executioner crawled back the way he had come. His knife clicked open, and he slashed the plastic tenting around the gangway. Heat was already pulsing through the metal floor in waves just above his head as he slid beneath the trailer. Bolan rolled out and came up into the tail end of a mob of people. Some were running toward the trailer and yelling *"Profesor! Profesor!"* and calling for water to put out the fire. Cooler heads were screaming to stay the hell away from it and let it burn.

Bolan raced back to the helicopter.

People were piling out of the little house, Castanado and Grimaldi among them. They were surrounded by men pointing guns at them. The leader of the camp was a short angry-looking man, and he whirled on them. The camp leader waved his arms and screamed, looking back and forth between them and the burning trailer. No one was paying much attention to the broken, blood-stained man who could barely stand.

Javier drew the Smith & Wesson Centennial Bolan had given him from his pocket and drilled the camp leader between the eyes at point-blank range. He shot the guard next to him in the same fashion before a burst from an AK-47 dropped him to the ground. Bolan raised his AK-47 and shot the two guards on either side of his men.

Guns began going off in all directions.

Grimaldi's .45 MAC-10 began snarling off bursts, and Castanado took aim with his Glock. Bolan pulled two baseball-shaped minifrags from his coat pocket and popped the pins. The mob of men around the trailer turned at the sound of gunfire and the two grenades landed among them. They shouted in sudden horror and then screamed as the bombs exploded.

A trail of bullets ripped up turf in a line just past Bolan as the machine gun in the tower tracked him. Bolan rolled away and came up firing until the AK racked open on an empty chamber. He tossed away the spent rifle and drew his pistols.

The machine gunner swung his weapon on Bolan but never got the chance to fire. He jerked and shuddered as Cervantes burned a long burst into him from the chopper's open cabin. The machine gunner toppled over the rail with his weapon and fell thirty feet to ground. Cervantes immediately felled the second man in the tower.

The survivors of the smuggling camp were fleeing for the hills. Bolan counted about six. The rest lay dead or wounded about the camp. Castanado and Grimaldi stood by the house surrounded by an arc of bodies. The pilot knelt by Javier. He pressed his hands over his wounds and grimaced at Bolan, who trotted up. It was bad. Javier had taken three rifle rounds through the belly.

"We gotta get him out of here, or he's going to die," Grimaldi said.

Cervantes shouted in alarm. "Cooper! Plane!"

Bolan looked up at the mouth of the valley. A plane was coming in. It was a sky-blue de Havilland Otter. The aircraft was capable of carrying fourteen people plus cargo, and this one was fitted with pontoons for an amphibious landing. It was obviously Franco's ticket to an island off Belize guaranteed to be free from infection. What Franco didn't know was that he was inside a plague plane.

Bolan sprinted toward the guard tower. He yanked the machine gun away from the fallen gunner. The Madsen was a pre-WWII weapon. Its parts were forged rather than stamped, and with minimum maintenance continued to soldier on in forgotten, far corners of the world. It was built more like a giant rifle than a modern automatic weapon. Bolan stripped the massive, banana-shaped magazine from the top of the action and replaced it with a fresh one from the gunner's pouch. He racked the action and charged toward the landing strip.

The Otter's pilot had taken notice of the burning trailer and the bodies littering the camp and pulled out of his landing approach. He pulled right into Bolan's line of fire. The Executioner shouldered the heavy weapon and burned all thirty rounds into the oncoming nose of the plane.

The Otter roared overhead, and Bolan was gratified to see black smoke suddenly spew out of the engine from both sides. The plane turned slowly and resumed its descent.

Grimaldi and Castanado scooped up Javier and ran for their lives as the plane plowed into the house. The clay roof crumbled, and the wings snapped off as the cockpit and cabin violently invaded the dwelling. The remaining walls collapsed onto the fallen aircraft, and dust and smoke oozed out of the rubble.

Bolan set down the machine gun and drew his pistol. Cervantes ran up from the chopper. "Where are you going?"

Bolan ignored the question. "Jack, get me a Willie Pete from the chopper."

"You got it."

Bolan clambered into the rubble. The plane was twisted and folded wreckage, but it was twisted, folded and infected wreckage. Bolan checked for survivors but found none. The seven men inside, including Franco, were in no better shape than the aircraft.

Soledad Korda was not among them.

Bolan stood and Grimaldi tossed the white-phosphorous grenade to him. The Executioner pulled the pin and shoved the grenade into the destroyed fuselage. He clambered out of the rubble and ran as streamers of white smoke and burning element shrieked out of every available hole in the plane. Bolan climbed the ladder to the tower and retrieved six spare magazines for the Madsen.

The men had loaded Javier into the chopper, and Cervantes was applying field dressings. Bolan slung the Madsen and clambered into the cabin.

"Jack, get us out of here," he said.

17

Bolan tapped Grimaldi's shoulder. "How soon until we're in Honduran airspace?"

The pilot shouted back over the rotor noise, "This area of the border is disputed! But official, undisputed Honduran airspace can't be more than—" he glanced at his map "—a minute away! Two at most! Why?"

"We have fast movers!" Bolan pointed. "Coming out of El Salvador!"

Grimaldi glanced backward.

"Shit!" he exclaimed.

"Yeah, that's what I figured!" Bolan agreed.

"El Salvador doesn't have the time or the money to patrol their airspace! Someone vectored these assholes in on us deliberately. They aren't making contact, so I don't think this is official business," the ace pilot shouted.

Javier wheezed from where he lay on the cabin floor, "The colonel, he has pilots in his pay. He has used the air force against his enemies before."

Bolan took a cargo strap and looped it around the base of the Madsen's barrel and clicked the other end to a cleat in the ceiling. "Here they come!"

The lead plane screamed with fire rippling beneath its wings. Bolan nearly fell out of the helicopter as it shifted to one side. He could feel the hot wave of the exhaust and smell the stink of propellant as the 2.75-inch rockets hissed past a few feet from the cabin. The jet screamed by a second later.

Grimaldi slewed the helicopter sideways and gave Bolan the second airplane in a straight fly-away profile. The Madsen hammered against Bolan's shoulder at four hundred rounds a minute. He was rewarded by the flash of hits on the enemy fuselage, and the jet ripped into a hard evasive turn. Grimaldi shifted the helicopter again as the wingman came in with his minigun spitting flame. Bullets tore through the helicopter's tail. The pair of jets screamed out of range and began banking to make another attack run.

"This isn't good!" Grimaldi shouted.

"Candy! Take the machine gun!" Bolan shouted as he dropped the Madsen on its sling and grabbed his rifle.

Cervantes was appalled. "Maybe I should—"

"Do it! Just shoot at any plane you can see!" Bolan checked the load in the M-203 beneath the barrel. It was a frag. He didn't have the time to go dig for an antiarmor round. "Jack, I need you to sucker one of them around to starboard!"

Cervantes was aft with the machine gun, and Grimaldi picked up the strategy instantly. He dropped the nose and dived hard toward the deck. The jets came screaming in. The Madsen hammered as Cervantes tried to put one of them in her sights. The wingman broke off to sweep in toward the chopper's unarmed side. Bolan crouched in the cabin with his carbine. His plan paid off.

Grimaldi was grinning. "Wingman never abandons his lead, asshole!"

The wingman came screaming in, aiming to get close to rake the chopper with his rockets. Grimaldi banked the helicopter in a vicious turn that left the broad side of the chopper open to the attack. It also brought the jet in a straight-on configuration. The grenade launcher thudded, and the spin-stabilized grenade flew straight at the jet's nose and was sucked into the starboard air intake. Flame blasted out of the engine from both ends.

"Hold on!" Grimaldi roared.

Bullets ripped through the chopper as the lead plane continued his gun run. His wingman tore past belching smoke and fire. The chopper spun as the jet wash of the passing plane hit it like a hammer. Grimaldi fought for control of his bird as alarms and warning lights howled and blinked in the cockpit. The lead jet was already soaring far ahead and banking around. The wingman was on fire and falling out of the sky. The bubble cockpit blasted open, and the twin seats erupted as the pilot and his weapons officer ejected.

"Sarge!" Grimaldi shouted over the bedlam. "I'm losing power!"

"Javier is hit!" Castanado shouted.

There wasn't much Bolan could do about either at the moment. The smell of smoke and burning oil joined the maelstrom of wind in the cabin. Something began clanking overhead in the engine compartment.

"Either I set her down, or we go down! You want me to milk an extra mile or two out of it?" Grimaldi asked.

"No! Put her down now!" Bolan kept his eye on the other jet. It had climbed for altitude and was observing the smoking helicopter land. The border landscape was a series of low rolling mountains and valleys. The chopper's skids crunched into river rock as Grimaldi brought them down beside a stream. Cervantes was still behind the Madsen glaring up at the sky. Bolan took a knee beside Javier.

The Black Shadow captain was dying.

"Candy, what's our friend doing?" Bolan doing.

"He's circling, up high, probably getting ready to do a rocket run."

"No," Javier gasped. "You shot down his friend. He won't come down and fight you. He will..." A fit of bloody, agonized coughing interrupted him.

"He's going to stay on station and vector in the helicopters," Bolan said.

"Yes."

Bolan knew it wouldn't take long. They needed to get under the cover of some trees.

"I'm not going to make it...and you can't carry me," Javier said.

Bolan shook his head. "No."

Javier grinned past bloody teeth. "You remember the day we met?"

"Yeah." Bolan grinned back. "Like it was yesterday."

"Then give me a grenade."

Bolan reached into a gear bag and pulled out one of his surplus pineapple grenades. He pulled the pin and pressed the grenade into Javier's hand. "*Vaya con dios,* Javier."

Javier gave a bloody croaking laugh. "I will go to hell for the things I have done." His eyes turned fierce despite his pain. "You just the send the colonel to join me. Go!"

Bolan handed his rifle to Cervantes and eyed the circling jet as he unslung the machine gun. They needed to find some cover.

ROTORS HAMMERED the sky. Bolan counted three before he could see them. Cervantes lay next to Bolan in a culvert a hundred yards from their abandoned helicopter. "You know the plane saw us come in here."

"Yeah," Bolan agreed.

"So...shouldn't we like, run, or something?"

"You can't outrun a helicopter. Besides, Billy still has a wounded leg. He'd be lamed in less than a mile. We'd have to leave him behind or put him down."

The young man's eyes widened at Bolan.

Bolan grinned. "I don't consider either an option."

"So...what's the plan," he asked.

"We need a helicopter."

Cervantes snorted. "Maybe one will pop up."

Bolan lifted his chin toward the creek as the helicopters crested the horizon. "Three just did."

Her smile grew predatory. "We're going to take one of theirs."

"Oh, yeah." Bolan watched as the helicopters came over the horizon. "Billy, give me my rifle."

"Which one?" They'd abandoned the helicopter, but Grimaldi had flown into El Salvador with an arsenal. Castanado was only good with a pistol, so he had been demoted to spear-carrier until things got close.

"The one on your left shoulder," Bolan said.

The young man handed Bolan a Steyr Scout Tactical rifle. The scope was set forward of the action, allowing the user to keep both eyes open for binocular vision. It was a concept Bolan heartily approved of. It was not a sniper rifle, per se, but more the weapon of the sharpshooter who needed very rapid, very accurate and very reliable fire in a running fight.

Bolan could take clay pigeons with one.

The three helicopters swept down into the little valley. They were painted olive drab and had door gunners hanging out of the cabins by chicken straps and cradling M-60 machine guns. They flew down in vee formation and landed to surround the fallen chopper on three sides. Men spilled out in all directions and put Grimaldi's downed bird in a cross fire. Most of the men wore fatigues and carried their M-16s like soldiers. They were not city slick kidnappers and leg breakers. These were the foot soldiers La Sombra Negra sent against armed enemy villages.

Bolan watched a man get out of the lead chopper's copilot seat. He was short, skinny and decidedly Central American Indian, but he wore a khaki uniform with muted captain's bars on the collar. His almond-shaped eyes gazed around the valley and stared into the culvert as if he could see the team where they were hiding. Bolan had spoken with Javier at some length in the night about the Black Shadow organization. He knew this man had to be Captain Joaquin Erasmo. He was one of Clellando's best officers and a hardened veteran of guerrilla warfare. He knifed his hand in the air, and six men spread out and surrounded the helicopter. Two of the men jumped into the open cabin from either side and one shouted back happily in Spanish. "It's Javier! He's alive! The traitor is alive!"

Erasmo roared with battle-won instincts. "Get back!"

The soldier drew his knife with a leer. "He is—"

The interior of the helicopter lit up with a bright flash and crack. The six men clustered around the open cabin screamed as chunks of crenellated iron tore mercilessly through their flesh. Bolan put his crosshairs on Erasmo and fired.

Erasmo stared in shock as the bullet took his left arm off at the elbow. His knees buckled beneath him and he sat down hard.

Erasmo's men knew they were in an ambush, and they had been trained to break it by charging down its throat. They came forward spraying from the hip. But, with the grenade's blast, they had not seen where Bolan's shot had come from.

"Candy, pull the string…" Bolan watched the men run into the zone along the creek he'd mentally mapped. "Now!"

Bolan's combat stores had included a hundred feet of parachute cord. The old Madsen had a bipod under the barrel and a monopod under the butt. Bolan had pushed the mono and bipod legs deep into the rocky soil to put the machine gun in a fixed line of fire and attached the cord around the trigger.

Cervantes pulled on the string. The Madsen snarled off a burst, and two men fell as the line of bullets intercepted them. Erasmo's men dropped or knelt and put a hailstorm of fire into the position, but for a few critical moments they would not be aware that they were engaging a piece of string.

"Give them another burst."

Cervantes pulled the string and the Madsen hammered. Bolan set down the Scout and picked up his carbine. He spoke quietly into his com link over the roar of automatic rifle fire. "Jack, are you in position?"

"Just about, give me five more minutes."

Cervantes snarled and held up the limp cord. "Shit!" A stray bullet had severed it.

Bolan peered through his sight and could see the enemy commander in the far helicopter. The Executioner knew if Erasmo was any kind of commander at all, Bolan and his little band were about to get pounded.

"Jack, you gotta go now!"

CAPTAIN ERASMO STARED at his arm again. Two of his men had dragged him back to the helicopter, and his personal medic was binding his wound. Erasmo had been a jungle fighter for twenty years, and his training cut through the shock. He quickly surveyed the battlefield. The enemy machine gun had fallen silent. The enemy was trying to suck them in and drag his men through a fighting retreat gauntlet of traps and sniper fire. If the enemy had blown off his head rather than his arm, he knew his lieutenant would probably have fallen for it hook, line and sinker.

"Bucho!" Erasmo boomed. The effort of shouting made his stump pulse with pain. "Bucho! Pull the men back!"

His first lieutenant glanced back from his rifle. His arm had been half raised to send everyone forward. "But we—"

Erasmo jerked back inside the cabin as he heard the unmistakable sound of a 40 mm grenade launcher.

Erasmo smiled savagely despite his wound and despite the fact that the grenade detonated twenty yards away and shredded four of his men. He'd had boxcar loads of grenades fired at him over the years, and by the sound he knew exactly where the enemy was. Erasmo snarled and pointed with his remaining hand. "The culvert! They are in the goddamn culvert!"

"*Sí, Capitán!*"

Bucho didn't see at all.

"Get that fighter pilot on the radio! Tell him to get his coward ass down on the deck! I want a rocket run on the culvert! I want an inferno in there! Then, gun runs until the asshole is out of ammo!"

"*Sí, Capitán!*"

"Put eight men in helicopter number two. Put them behind the culvert. Have the door gunners dismount the machine guns. Close their back door!"

"*Sí, Capitán!*"

"Get helicopter number one in the air! I want them orbiting the culvert! Low enough so the door gunners can see any muzzle-flash and fire on it!"

"*Sí, Capitán!*"

Erasmo was impressed. When he had seen the abandoned chopper, he was sure the American was making a run for the Honduran border. Not that that would have saved him. Instead, he had attacked, but it would not be enough. Javier was dead, and all the American had was a woman, a boy and a pilot.

They would be overwhelmed.

"Bucho, get your—"

"Capitán!" Bucho was raising his rifle. He stopped as the front of his shirt filled with bullet strikes. The helicopter door gunners sagged in their straps, one either side of Erasmo, and so did the two men guarding him. The medic was staring in horror. Erasmo followed his look. He tried to draw his pistol but only managed to flap his stump.

A mud man stood beside the helicopter. Every inch of him was covered with brown mud, black slime and green algae. The only part of him not coated with filth was the sound-suppressed MAC-10 submachine gun in his hand. Erasmo's heart sank. He had been suckered. The helicopter landed by the creek had been bait, and this man had sprung the American commando's real trap.

The mud mask split into a startling grin. "I am prepared to accept your surrender."

The Executioner thought about Belize and about the information Erasmo had given them. The tiny former British colony had almost nothing in common with the rest of Central America. The republic was relatively free of crime, coups and civil wars. Correspondingly, Bolan had never spent a whole lot of time there. Grimaldi, on the other hand, had an almost encyclopedic knowledge of places you could land a plane on planet Earth. "Jack, is Punta Gorda an international airport?"

The mud man turned in the pilot's seat. There had been no time to clean him up. The pilot grinned through his flaking mud mask and shouted over the rotors. "No! Belize doesn't have a rail system, so they're dependent on small planes for domestic transport. Lots of little airports and landing strips all over the place. I know a lot of ex-patriot American and European pilots who come down here for puddle-jumping jobs. Everyone around here speaks English and the currency is stable. It's a good gig! Hell, I might retire here!"

"What's the international airport?"

"BZE in Ladyville! About ten minutes outside of Belize City! On the coast!"

"What cities do international flights hub in through?"

"Los Angeles, Dallas and Miami, usually!"

Bolan's thoughts traveled back to the map on the wall of Drayton's bio lab. Miami, Dallas and L.A. had been surrounded by concentric rings of infection that spread across the United States in interlocking ripples with red lines arcing out to points all across the planet. "They won't be going straight to Punta Gorda! They'll either have an agent or an aerosol dispersal device set on a timer aboard a flight to each city! Get on the horn to the Farm! Tell Hal that Miami International, Dallas-Forth Worth and LAX are the planned infection points. Any flight out of Belize City entering U.S. airspace must be forced down and quarantined or shot down. He'd better tell the President to notify Mexico in case they try to divert. Tell him he'd better get on the horn with Belize in case they try to turn back!"

"I'm on it! Where do you want to go?"

"Belize City. I don't think we're too far behind the colonel. I want to stop the outbreak before it starts."

Belize International Airport, Ladyville

BZE WAS THE CLASSICAL, sleepy two-room third world airport. The six gates were all in the communal departure area, and the gates themselves were just glass doors that opened to the tarmac. As Grimaldi had said, most of the flights were small prop planes bound for spots along the coast or the interior. There was a surprisingly large number of people in the terminal. It was the height of the tourist season. The vast majority of the waiting passengers were sleek and tan Americans and Europeans wearing technical outdoor clothing. There was very little in the way of amenities save for a cafeteria and an open-air observation deck, so most people spent their time watching the other people.

Bolan drew more glances than he cared for.

He had cleaned up as much as possible, but his suit had been in two battles. The knees and cuffs were stained with dirt and grass. The jacket had been repeatedly splashed with other people's blood, and he'd been forced to abandon it. That meant he'd had to abandon his shoulder rig and big guns, as well. He had one of his Centennials in his pocket and the other in an ankle holster. Cervantes's backup piece was a snub-nosed Smith & Wesson Bodyguard, and Bolan had commandeered it. Grimaldi was covered with mud, and Cervantes was still wearing her raid suit. They were ready and waiting in the helicopter. Castanado had limped in a minute or two after Bolan had taken a seat and tried to look innocuous.

Bolan glanced at the list of international flights. There were only three, and they were timed close together. They were due to leave for Miami, Dallas and

Los Angeles each about half an hour apart. The flight for Miami was leaving shortly.

"Can I help you, love?" Bolan was somewhat sweaty and disheveled, but by the way the Creole girl behind the reservations counter was smiling it was pretty obvious she thought he would clean up okay.

Bolan glanced at her name tag and decided to use the direct approach. He'd never seen Salah Samman, but Soledad Korda had given him a good description. "Yeah, Chloe, perhaps you can. I'm supposed to meet a friend of mine here. Long black hair, tan, dresses flash and too good-looking for his own good?"

Chloe smiled. "I believe he's freshening up."

"Thanks." Bolan stepped away and clicked open his phone while the woman beamed after him. He glanced at the men's room. A man was standing outside trying to read a newspaper and act casual, but he was clearly a lookout. Bolan could make out the bulge of the pistol under his left armpit. "Jack, I need you to run a recon on the men's room. Samman may be inside. Possibly with accomplices."

"You got it."

Grimaldi jumped out of the chopper and trotted down the tarmac. Just about every eye in the terminal turned his way as he came through the glass door. Dirt and dust flaked away from him with every step, and the ropes of algae festooning him had hardened to the consistency of a bird's nest. He walked past Bolan and straight toward Chloe.

He tossed off his most devilish smile. "The Roaring Creek river tour?" He waggled his crusted eyebrows at Chloe. "Don't do it."

Chloe giggled despite her initial revulsion.

"Listen, I have to be on a plane in an hour, and I really need to use your facilities."

"Well, so I might imagine, love." Chloe agreed. "To the left of the baggage carousel."

"Thanks."

Grimaldi sauntered off to the men's room greeting every stare with a devil-may-care grin. The sentry was wearing sunglasses, but Grimaldi could feel his eyes on him. The sentry shifted his feet and kicked one heel against the door. The pilot ignored him and walked in.

Salah Samman stood at the sinks. There were eight men in the lavatory, and they were clearly together. Three of them, including Samman, had shaving kits on the counter, and all three were zipping them up. Grimaldi gave the wanted terrorist a rueful smile. "You wouldn't believe the day I've had," he said lightly.

No one was smiling.

Grimaldi glanced around to make sure there were no feet beneath the stalls and marked the faces of Samman's men. "The Roaring Creek river tour?" he repeated with a sheepish smile. "Don't do it, man. Not before a flight."

Samman's black eyes were fixed on Grimaldi with

dark intensity. His men's hands hovered near their concealed pistols.

Grimaldi took an intimidated step back. "Uh...listen, I'm probably going to make this place a mess and use up all the soap, so...why don't you guys finish up first."

Samman's lips twisted into a thin smile. "That would be very kind of you."

"Okay, well, um, let me know when you're done and—"

"You may go now," Samman said.

Grimaldi dropped his gaze fearfully to his feet and hurried out. He could feel the sentry's eyes on his back. He turned to a porter. "Is there a hose around here I can use?"

The porter jerked his head toward the nearest gate. "There's a faucet just outside."

Grimaldi went outside and clicked open his phone and pressed conference call. "Sarge, I count eight including two knuckleheads who look like they can bench press the planet. They're all packing heat, but they didn't seem like soldiers or cops. I think they're MS rather than death squad guys. Your boy Samman is in there, and I can't swear to it but I'm betting they have three of those aerosol dispersal devices you were talking about in their shaving kits on the counter. I think they're prepping them now."

"Good work. Get back to the chopper and gear up. This is going to get hectic real fast," Bolan said.

Cervantes spoke over the line. "Cooper, Captain Erasmo wants in. He wants a gun."

Bolan sat in a cafeteria chair with a copy of the *San Pedro Sun* in front of him. Eight. It was an ugly number. For a tiny Central American airport, there were far too many innocent friendlies around and three virulent bombs ready to go off and no quarantine in effect. The fact was Bolan needed every gun. "Is he lucid?"

"I was going to give him another shot of morphine while we were waiting, but he refused. I'd say he's pretty goddamn salty."

Bolan had interrogated Erasmo and was convinced he was unaware of and horrified by Clellando's plan. "Bind his arm tight and give him back his pistol."

He turned to Castanado. "Billy, be ready. This is about to go down," he whispered.

A voice over the loudspeaker announced that Flight 57 to Miami would begin boarding in ten minutes. Salah Samman came out of the men's room surrounded by a phalanx of men.

"Showtime." Bolan clicked his phone shut and filled each hand with a snub-nosed 9 mm pistol. Out on the tarmac, he could see Grimaldi, Cervantes and Erasmo coming in at a run. People on the observation deck noticed the armed trio as well. Samman lifted his head, and his hand drifted under his jacket.

"Samman!" Bolan boomed. Samman froze for a split second, and the little revolver in Bolan's hand barked.

A bodyguard shoved Samman aside and put a wall of muscle between him and Bolan's bullet. Everyone in the terminal began screaming and running in all directions.

"Down! Everyone down!" Bolan roared. A few people dropped and cowered, but the majority of the travelers continued screaming and running in panic. One of Samman's men was bellowing at Castanado in Spanish. "Billy C! You traitor! I'll kill you!"

The gleaming Colt Python in his hand roared and smashed a hapless porter to the ground. Castanado held his Glock in a two-handed stance and popped off shots between running figures. He desperately flipped his selector to full-auto as the big man closed in and clamped down the trigger. The machine pistol walked a 10-round burst point-blank up the bodyguard's body from his crotch to his forehead.

Bolan shot down two more of Samman's men, and his little revolver clicked empty. His left-hand pistol rose as Samman produced the tapering shape of a Turkish Zigana pistol and yanked a screaming woman before him as a shield.

Grimaldi, Cervantes and Erasmo burst into the terminal and everyone began shooting at once. Glass shattered behind Erasmo in a crashing cascade as his opponent missed his head by inches. The captain stood unflinchingly and fired his .45 one-handed, and his opponent fell with his face in ruins. Salah's remaining man fled toward the farthest gate, but Bolan put two bullets between his shoulder blades and he pitched forward and sprawled into the baggage carousel. Samman took advantage of his human shield to shoot at Cervantes and Castanado. The woman staggered but she was wearing full body armor over her raidsuit. The young fighter's pistol fell from his hands in a spray of blood, and he stared at himself incredulously. The bullet had blown away the middle, ring and little fingers of his left hand and traveled on in a bloody furrow up his right arm to his shoulder.

He turned white and sat down, blinking in shock. Neither Grimaldi nor Erasmo had a shot.

Bolan charged.

He only had one bullet left in his pistol, and he had to get close to Samman to take the head shot with a snub-nosed revolver. Samman caught Bolan's motion and grinned as he leveled his pistol past his hostage's head. The black eye of the muzzle stared directly at Bolan. He felt the trip-hammer blows slamming into his chest.

Samman's eyes widened as he realized his opponent wore armor under his clothes. The Turkish pistol rose for Bolan's head. The hostage screamed as Bolan thrust the little revolver three feet in front of her head and fired.

Samman released his hostage as he convulsed backward. The hostage broke away howling and sobbing as Bolan dived into his opponent. He grabbed Samman's carry-on and pulled out the shaving kit. Inside was a gleaming stainless-steel cylinder the size and shape of a paratrooper's bail-out bottle. A digital timer was set in the casing and a multinozzled spigot protruded from one end. The timer was counting down and was currently at one hour and fifty-seven minutes.

Samman struggled to get up.

"Lay still." Bolan put his knee into Samman's chest and pinned him. "I'll get you help."

Samman's hand darted to his watch. "Fuck you."

Samman's thumb pressed the bezel with an audible click, and the timer on the cylinder made a terrible electronic peep in answer. The gun barked once in Bolan's hand, and Samman slumped over dead.

Bolan went cold as he looked at the timer on the cylinder. It was now at fifty-seven seconds and counting down.

"There are two more cylinders! Find them! Go! Go! Go!" he shouted.

Cervantes and Grimaldi charged forward. They began stripping bodies of their carry-ons and ripping them open.

"Found one!" Cervantes shoved a gleaming cylinder at Bolan. Its timer was synchronized with the first and it was at forty seconds.

"I don't see it!" Grimaldi bounded from body to body. "I don't see it!"

Bolan ran to the man he'd put down on the carousel.

He moaned as Bolan flipped him over and ripped the bag off his arm. Bolan found the shaving kit and the cylinder inside.

Thirty seconds.

The terminal was full of cowering fearful tourists and airport employees, some of them wounded. Bolan had only three effectives on his team and no way to enforce a quarantine on an airport.

Twenty seconds.

Bolan caught the scent of food cooking and sprinted for the cafeteria.

Two cafeteria girls screamed as he hurdled the counter. He hit a slick spot on the tiled floor and fell, a steel cylinder clanging away as it squirted out of his grasp. He clawed his way to his feet and scooped up the bomb.

Five seconds.

He wasn't going to make the refrigerator in the back. Two cooks stood in front of it cornered with nowhere to go.

The counter girls screamed as Bolan hurled the cylinders into the deep fat fryer. The fryer made a noise like a steam engine and french fries and boiling oil flew in all directions. Bolan elbowed a sink spigot and plunged his scalded hands under the cold water. He glanced back at the fryer. It crackled and roiled in golden brown waves and continued to hiss as if in anger at its new and unnatural burden. Bolan checked the thermometer. The virus had been plunged into a 360-degree environment.

Bolan was fairly sure he'd achieved containment.

Grimaldi hopped over the counter and eyeballed the situation. "You do it in time?"

"Yeah, I think so."

"Deep fried smallpox." The pilot grinned. "You know there's a pun there somewhere but I can't find it."

Bolan wasn't laughing.

Grimaldi sighed. "You ain't laughing."

"I'm thinking Clellando is the kind of guy to keep a little something on the side for insurance." Bolan pulled his hands out of the sink. "We have one more stop to make."

19

"ETA five minutes, Striker." The helicopter thundered over the sea. The sun was dropping like a stone, and the purple water scant feet beneath the skids churned into golden foam in their rotor wash. Things had moved pretty fast and furiously at the airport in Belize. The United States government had spent the past forty-eight hours preparing for some kind of outbreak in Central America. Reinforced Special Forces teams had been sent to the Salvadoran and Honduran capitals. Belize had come out of the blue, but fortunately the President had put in a call to the British prime minister. The British maintained an Army Training and Support Unit to ostensibly maintain Belizean sovereignty against her somewhat unstable and war-torn neighbors. They had thrown a cordon around the airport. Bolan was certain the virus had been contained, but no one was taking his word for it. It would take days to test everyone at the airport. Bolan and his team had slipped away, but their orders were strict. They were not to land again unless they found the mystery island.

The Belize government had not been made aware of this. It had been decided that coordinating with them would take too long and would give Clellando too much time to act. Bolan and his team were still a go. It wasn't much of a team. Two of them had been shot, and all five were exhausted. Grimaldi had taken the opportunity to hose off on the tarmac and looked like a reasonable facsimile of his usual self.

They were running low on fuel, and this was the third of the most likely islands they were checking. Grimaldi skimmed in low.

"There!" Cervantes pointed.

The island was kidney shaped and dark green in the failing light, but a pier was visible sticking out of a chunk of the jungle. Set just under the trees was pair of large, prefab boat sheds almost overgrown with trees and vegetation. It was a deliberate camouflage job and explained why satellites had shown little. A pair of Sea Otter prop planes occupied the sheds as well a speedboat and a larger fishing launch.

"You want me to take us in for a closer look?" Grimaldi asked.

Bolan knew Clellando had to have heard their rotors. If he had spies anywhere in Belize, he would also have to know that something had gone terribly wrong with the plan at the airport. Bolan's thoughts were confirmed as a pair of jeeps appeared out of the forest. He scanned them through his binoculars. Clellando was in the lead vehicle. Each one had four men. They were all carrying M-16 rifles.

"Take us in closer. Keep us out of rifle range," Bolan said.

The jeeps ground to a halt in the sand. Clellando stepped out of his vehicle and set down his rifle. He picked up a stick with one end wrapped in fabric and a pair of binoculars. He stepped out onto the little pier by himself. Bolan and the colonel regarded each other through their optics. The colonel waved the stick. The handkerchief unfurled.

Clellando was waving a white flag.

Clellando was a military man. He had to know that he was the most wanted man on Earth. U.S. and British intelligence would never stop hunting him. Bolan had no doubt Clellando had kept a sample of the virus. He also had Soledad Korda. He'd know negotiating with Bolan would be easier than dealing with the sweep-and-destroy mission Delta Force would be launching within the next few hours.

But Bolan wasn't buying the white flag.

"Missile!" Erasmo shouted.

Bolan caught the yellow flash of fire illuminating the interior of one of the boathouses. The missile hurtled out of the shed like a green dart on the impulse of its booster charge. A second later the missile's main rocket motor screamed into life and the weapon went supersonic.

Grimaldi flew straight into the missile's arc in an attempt to turn it. He shouted over the rotors with dead certainty. "We're not going to make it!"

"Bail out!" Bolan shouted.

Castanado held up his bandaged hands in sudden terror. "I can't—"

Bolan grabbed him, scooped up his rifle and dived out over the skid. The Caribbean Sea slammed into them like a sweat-hot hammer. The younger man lost his rifle as he tumbled. Bolan curled into a ball, and the second he stopped skipping he dived down into the depths. Castanado was sinking like a stone, trailing bubbles into the murk. Bolan slid his arm around the young man's shoulder and neck and began the torturous task of kicking his way back up carrying airless deadweight.

The Executioner paused as the surface of the sea above lit up in an orange flash. His lungs burned as he kicked to stay in place. A vast burning bulk hit the water some hundred yards distant. Bits of wreckage rained against the surface and sunk, bubbling and sizzling, to the bottom. Bolan forced himself to wait for several more lung-burning seconds. His caution was rewarded as an eight-foot section of rotor hit the water almost directly overhead and scythed down like a slow-motion saber into the depths.

Bolan kicked upward as lights began to dance around his vision, and he broke the surface with a ragged gasp.

He immediately began scissor kicking and stroking for shore with his free arm. Bolan ignored the retching sounds. Dead men didn't vomit, and the ragged gasps between implied the young man was breathing.

He heard the crackle of rifle fire from the shore. Clellando and his men were laughing as they took shots. Eight hundred yards was long range for men with iron sights firing free hand. Bolan swam for the outer tip of the kidney-shaped island to put it between him and the gunmen. He could see Cervantes and Erasmo struggling for shore ahead of him. The tiny strip of sand seemed like a million miles away, but the incoming tide was on his side. He began to grow concerned when the shooting stopped, and he heard the two jeeps fire up their engines.

They'd burned far too much time.

Bolan caught up with Cervantes and Erasmo as his feet hit the sandy bottom. The four of them slogged onto the beach. Grimaldi was already on the beach, cleaner than he'd been in hours and cussing up a storm. The pilot had crashed and had more aircraft shot out from under him than anyone could count. He still considered it a personal insult every time.

He tapered off cursing as the rest of the team reached the beach. "Took you guys long enough."

Bolan dropped his burden. Castanado fell facedown into the sand, gasping. Erasmo was a veteran jungle fighter, but he'd lost an arm and been in two gunfights in the past twenty-four hours. Even with help, the long swim had nearly killed him. Cervantes was gray with exhaustion, but she'd retained her MP-5.

Bolan hauled Castanado to his feet and pressed his Beretta into the young man's hand. "Stand up, breathe, keep it on semiauto."

Castanado nodded. He looked like the evening breeze would push him over.

"They are coming," Erasmo observed.

Bolan had heard the approaching engines as well. Clellando had obviously hoped to intercept them before they had reached the shore and shoot them like ducks in a barrel.

Bolan heard the grinding of gears. It appeared there was no road on this side of the island, and Clellando and his men were crunching their way through the tropical terrain.

Bolan drew the Desert Eagle and held out his free hand to Cervantes. "Give me your ten."

She slapped the big Smith & Wesson into Bolan's palm and followed it with four spare magazines. "Form a skirmish line, ten yards apart, start moving forward when you hear me shoot."

Bolan loped into the trees. It wasn't quite a mangrove swamp or tropical jungle, but the island foliage was thick enough, and beneath the canopy it was already growing dark. Bolan moved at a crouch and then crawled as he caught sight of the lead jeep.

Both vehicles plowed through the underbrush, weaving between the larger trees and crushing the saplings. Bolan burst out of the giant ferns and took a flying step up onto the driver's-side fender. The driver had a moment to scream as the 10 mm pistol blasted in Bolan's hand and shot the passenger. The .44 Magnum Desert Eagle boomed in Bolan's right to pulverize the two men in the back. The driver clawed for his weapon and flailed against his seat as the two huge pistols put holes through his chest.

Bolan dropped back to the sandy ground, and a corpse fell from the back seat as the second vehicle lurched to a halt. Rifle fire crackled and struck the first jeep, tearing through the corpses. Bolan stripped the body of its rifle and six spare magazines and crawled wide through the underbrush as bullets cracked overhead.

The colonel had not been in either jeep.

Submachine guns opened up from the shore, and the men in the jeep returned a storm of automatic fire.

Bolan sighted down his pirated M-16, and as he fired, his target toppled out the back. The passenger leaped out, but Grimaldi and Cervantes caught him in a cross fire that spun him to the sand. Bolan ran in a wide circle as the driver rammed the jeep into reverse. He paused to shoot the other man out of the back. The driver tried to drive, look behind him and spray at Bolan one-handed with his rifle. The Executioner dropped to one knee and flipped his weapon to full-auto. He lowered his sights and fired. The driver cried out as the foot well of the jeep swarmed with full-metal-jacketed bullets. The jeep slammed to a stop against a tree, and the driver fell out the side howling and clutching his ruined calves.

"Clear!" Bolan rose and stalked to the jeep. The driver shrieked in fear at the M-16 in his face. "You speak English?" Bolan asked.

"Yes!"

"Where's the colonel?"

"Back! Back at the house!"

"With how many men?"

"A squad! Twelve men!" the terrified man replied.

"And the woman, Soledad Korda?"

"She is..." The man couldn't look Bolan in the face.

"She's what?"

"She is dead!" the gunman squeaked.

Bolan could imagine the kind of revenge the colonel had taken. These men had probably participated. They'd probably all taken their turn. By the same token, these eight men in the jeeps had been sacrificed. "You're Mara Salvatrucha?"

"Yes!"

"The colonel's men, in the house with him, all Sombra Negra?"

"I..." The wounded man considered this with dawning suspicion. "Yes."

Bolan frowned. He had just taken out Clellando's garbage for him. The colonel had known these men would not reach the beach in time and would most likely be slaughtered. They were a diversion. The million-dollar question was just what was Clellando up to? Logically he should be airborne already.

The colonel was waiting for something.

Bolan had a cold feeling the colonel was waiting for him.

20

"I don't like it," Grimaldi said, frowning at the house.

Bolan didn't like it, either. He squatted in the dark of the trees as clouds of mosquitoes rose around him. The architecture was English tropical Colonial rather than Spanish hacienda, with a broad lawn and a fountain. The lights were on, the welcome mat was out and no one was about. It stank of a trap. Bolan's heavy weapons and his night-vision gear had gone down to Davy Jones's locker with the helicopter. He was reduced to pistols and the pick of the litter of some poorly maintained Salvadoran civil war issue M-16 rifles bereft of optics or grenade launchers.

"Erasmo, what's he doing?"

The captain squatted against a tree. He couldn't seem to catch his breath. His stump was bleeding again. "The colonel? He learned from your Rangers. Stalk your stalkers. Ambush your ambushers."

"He has something up his sleeve," Bolan said.

"I would say several things."

Bolan cupped his hands to either side of his mouth and shouted at the house. "Colonel! Hand over the virus!"

The Executioner thought about mentioning the Delta teams already in the air coming to scrape the island clean, but Clellando would already know all about that. He had some kind of an out. He also had the advantage of position, numbers and firepower.

Claymores at the edge of the trees suddenly detonated in a ring around the house like a string of firecrackers. Bolan shoved Cervantes down as the antipersonnel mines hurled out thousands of steel ball bearings in interlocking fan-shaped arcs. The trees and underbrush withered under the storm of steel. Castanado twisted and fell, and Grimaldi went flying.

Bolan crawled to Castanado. The young man lay moaning, his arm bleeding. Cervantes got there first and packed a field dressing against it.

"Candy, they're going to be—"

Castanado groaned as Cervantes collapsed on top of him. Bolan pulled her off, and in the gloom he could see her head was covered with blood. Two long, bloody tracks scored her head along the top of her skull and just above her left ear. Bolan could see the gleam of bone in the starlight.

Half a dozen armed men came piling out of the house.

Bolan pressed a field dressing against Cervantes's

skull and laid her in the injured man's lap. He cinched the dressing around the young man's arm and pressed his pistol back into his hand. "Billy! Stay with her!"

Bolan searched the shredded foliage.

Grimaldi lay facedown in the dirt. Bolan rolled him over, and the pilot looked at him with an exhausted wheeze. The Claymore mine was like a giant shotgun shell. The round steel bearings it used as projectiles didn't have the power to penetrate body armor, but the pilot had taken about seven hundred of them in the chest at point-blank range. He hadn't been shredded, but his body had been forced to absorb a huge load of kinetic energy. He was pale and shaking and could only breathe in tiny, strangled sips of air.

"You all right?" Bolan asked.

Grimaldi made a palsied attempt to cock an eyebrow. "I'm...fucking...tip-top. You?"

Captain Erasmo crouched behind a tree with his .45 in his remaining hand. "They come," he said.

Bolan's team was just about done. He shoved Grimaldi's weapon back in his hands and crawled back to Castanado. "Count to five and cry out."

The Executioner faded back into the brush.

The young man didn't have to act to put pain and desperation into his wounded cry.

The gunmen beelined toward the voice, loping through the trees like wolves and spraying their M-16s as they came. Bolan rose, and his own M-16 hammered on full-auto. He put three bursts into three men before they could turn. He dropped back behind a tree as the remaining three fired back. Wood chips flew, but the tropical hardwood took the hits. The three men had been well trained. They charged Bolan's position firing suppressively. Erasmo stepped from behind his tree, and his pistol thudded twice. Two of the gunmen fell with .45 slugs in the back of their brains. The third man twisted around and fired back, but Erasmo had already disappeared into the shadows. The gunman's M-16 suddenly clacked open on empty.

Bolan reversed his rifle in his hand and came out from cover.

The man spun at the movement. He popped his spent magazine and clawed for a fresh one, but he was too late. His eyes bugged in horror as Bolan raised his rifle overhead like an ax.

Springs flew as Bolan shattered the stock of his rifle across the gunman's kneecaps. The man fell howling in pain. Bolan drew his Desert Eagle and stepped on the side of the screaming man's face to shut him up. "What's your name?"

The man grimaced against Bolan's boot. "Arcelio!"

"You want to live, Arcelio?"

"Yes!" Arcelio seemed pretty fervent about it.

"How many still in the house besides Clellando?"

"Six!"

The numbers were still adding up. That was one

good thing. "How are you and the colonel getting off the island?"

The man made a hesitant, mewling noise. Bolan stepped harder. "I asked you a question."

"Scuba!" the man shrieked.

That was interesting, and not a bad backup plan. The colonel knew once he'd seen Bolan's helicopter that satellites would soon be surveying his island. There would be no way he could take off in his planes without being spotted and tracked. However, the island was only a couple of miles offshore with no nearby towns or villages. The colonel and his men could easily swim to the uninhabited shore even under the nose of watching satellites. It would take sonar to detect them, and the U.S. didn't have any nuclear submarines off Belize. Clellando and his men were Ranger trained. They could easily march deep into the rain forest and lose themselves beneath the tropical canopy, make themselves a jungle encampment and lie around in hammocks eating barbecued sloth while they outwaited the plague.

"The colonel still has some of the virus?"

"Yes!"

"Here?"

"Yes. In the house."

That was about the only good news. Erasmo walked up, reloading his .45 by tucking it under his stump. "It is down to you and me."

"The colonel has six men still in the house, but he needs to finish us off before he goes swimming."

"We can hold him here until your Special Forces come. Yes?"

"I don't think he's going to wait that long."

Bolan picked up an extra rifle. "I wonder if he's land-mined the lawn?"

Erasmo picked up an M-16 and held it like a giant pistol. "I don't think he's had time."

"Then let's do it." Bolan flicked his selectors to full auto. "Go!"

The Executioner and Capitan Erasmo came out of the trees like Butch and Sundance breaking out of Bolivia. Bolan fired an M-16 in either hand. Erasmo joined in handling his rifle one-handed as best he could. They sprayed for suppressive effect rather than accuracy. The lawn was a killing zone, and there was no time to stop and aim.

They reached the veranda without a shot being fired in return and plastered themselves on either side of the front door. Erasmo was gasping like a flounder in the bottom of a boat. Bolan was on the ragged edge of exhaustion himself. He closed his eyes for one moment and vainly wished for a five-gallon bucket full of hand grenades.

He opened his eyes and wasn't surprised that they hadn't appeared and nor were they likely to anytime soon.

"The hell with this noise. Kick the door when I give the signal."

Bolan stepped away from the door and hurled one of his six-pound rifles through the shutter and the glass behind it. He crouched as he was rewarded by rifle fire screaming back out the shattered opening. He shoved his second rifle over the sill and fired blindly into the room beyond. "Now!"

Erasmo put foot to door and emptied the rest of his M-16 around the jamb. He dropped it as it clacked open on empty. He jumped back and drew his pistol, and the enemy assault rifles answered from inside. The thick brickwork stopped the bullets. Bolan moved to the next window and hurled his rifle through it. He fired the big Desert Eagle through the ruined aperture but no fire returned.

The shattered remnants of the windowpanes broke as Bolan dived through them. He rolled up with a pistol in each hand. Feet thudded in the hallway. The room he was in was unlit, but the hall was. The outer wall of the house was brick, but the inner walls were wood and plaster. Shadows flew across the open door into the hall, and Bolan's pistols rolled in his hands. The wallpaper cratered, and someone in the hall screamed and fell. Three men came through the door, guns blazing.

The first two fell beneath Bolan's pistols. Erasmo shoved his arm through the shattered window and shot the third in the head. Bolan kept his guns on the door, but no one else came pounding down the hallway. Erasmo crawled awkwardly through the window, his stump flapping like the wing of penguin. He fell to the floor with a thud and lay gasping. Bolan noted that the three fallen men were wearing wet suits. Erasmo leaned heavily on the wall to stand up. "Three more."

"And the colonel."

"*Sí*, and the colonel." Erasmo took a deep breath and shouted out in Spanish. "This is Captain Erasmo! You know me! All we want is Clellando!"

Silence greeted them.

"Just run away! Throw down your guns and run! I promise the American won't kill you!" Erasmo shook his head and muttered under his breath, "But I fucking will."

Feet pounded through the house. One man came running into the room, shooting wildly.

Erasmo's blast shook the paintings on the walls and the man collapsed.

"Now, two," Erasmo grunted, "plus the colonel."

Bolan stepped out into the hallway, moving past the foyer. He caught the scent of food from the kitchen and glanced up the staircase. Clellando wouldn't be the kind of man to tree himself. Then again he—

From upstairs Clellando shouted, "Now!"

A rifleman leaned out from the kitchen. Clellando and his other man leaned over the landing at the top of the stairs. Bolan swung up both pistols, turning like a turret as the rifles began firing. The burst from the rifleman at the top of the stairs went high and wide as Bolan's pistols rolled and thundered in his hands and hammered the man to pieces. Erasmo staggered as he took a bullet from the man in the kitchen but his right arm stayed rigidly on target, and he shot the man in the face with his .45. Clellando's shotgun detonated like doomsday, and Erasmo was swatted to the floor like a fly.

Bolan stared at the darkness at the top of the stairs. He thought he'd hit Clellando, but he couldn't tell. He kept his pistols trained upward as he took a knee beside Erasmo. The captain had taken the majority of a pattern of buckshot center body mass. He stared up glassily at Bolan. The captain's mouth worked as if he wanted to say something, but all that came was a gurgle. Capitan Joaquin Erasmo blinked and went slack as he bled out onto the tiles.

The Executioner rose and took time to reload his pistols. There was no particular hurry. He knew what he would find upstairs. Bolan walked up the stairs and down the hall to the open door of the master bedroom. Clellando stood by the window grinning. He was wearing a blue-and-gray wet suit, with a diving knife strapped to his calf. He was holding a Remington 870 pump shotgun with a fourteen-inch barrel.

Bolan lunged to one side and dropped. Clellando was a big man, but the shotgun weighed six pounds and was a very awkward weapon. The shotgun roared. Bolan felt the wind of the buckshot by his face, and the mirror behind him exploded. He ripped his boot knife free and flung it.

Bolan flung himself over the bed like an Olympic gymnast on a tumbling run.

The shotgun clacked as Clellando racked the action.

Bolan took an extra eye blink to steady his aim as the shotgun leveled for him. He shot Clellando twice in the face. The shotgun roared its final shot and Bolan felt buckshot hit his armored shoulder and burn across the exposed muscle of his upper arm. He ignored it and jumped to his feet. Clellando was tottering. Bolan lunged in, cocking back his hand, the spent pistol cupped in his palm to slap Clellando's skull.

The colonel finally fell.

Grimaldi's voice came barely above a whisper from the bedroom doorway. "Sarge?"

The pilot looked like death warmed over. Only the doorjamb kept him from falling over.

"We got him," Bolan said. "How are Candy and Billy?"

"Billy is okay. The bleeding is under control. You bound him up pretty good. Candy is unconscious, but I think she'll be okay."

"Can you fly?"

The pilot looked up at Bolan weakly. It was a bad day when Jack Grimaldi said no to that question. "I don't know. I think...my sternum's cracked or something."

"Sit down before you fall down. I'll call the Farm. Delta Force will be here soon."

The Executioner looked around. He knew that stopping Clellando was only a minor victory in his War Everlasting.

A drug lord attempts to exploit North America's appetite for oil... and cocaine

Don Pendleton's Mack Bolan
Ultimate Stakes

A double political kidnapping in Ecuador is cause for concern in the U.S. when the deed threatens a new and vital petroleum distribution agreement between the two countries. The question of who is behind the conspiracy and why turns grim when the trail leads to one of the biggest narcotraffickers in South America, a kingpin ruthlessly exploiting the demand for oil—and narcotics.

Available September 2006 wherever you buy books.

Or order your copy now by sending your name, address, zip or postal code, along with a check or money order (please do not send cash) for $6.50 for each book ordered ($7.99 in Canada), plus 75¢ postage and handling ($1.00 in Canada), payable to Gold Eagle Books, to:

In the U.S.
Gold Eagle Books
3010 Walden Avenue
P.O. Box 9077
Buffalo, NY 14269-9077

In Canada
Gold Eagle Books
P.O. Box 636
Fort Erie, Ontario
L2A 5X3

Please specify book title with your order.
Canadian residents add applicable federal and provincial taxes.

GSB110

James Axler
Outlanders

An ancient Chinese emperor stakes his own dark claim to Earth...

HYDRA'S RING

A sacred pyramid in China is invaded by what appears to be a ruthless Tong crime lord and his army. But a stunning artifact and a desperate summons for the Cerberus exiles put the true nature of the looming battle into horrifying perspective. Kane and his rebels must confront a four-thousand-year-old emperor, an evil entity as powerful as any nightmare now threatening humankind's future....

Available November 2006 wherever you buy books.

Or order your copy now by sending your name, address, zip or postal code, along with a check or money order (please do not send cash) for $6.50 for each book ordered ($7.99 in Canada), plus 75¢ postage and handling ($1.00 in Canada), payable to Gold Eagle Books, to:

In the U.S.
Gold Eagle Books
3010 Walden Avenue
P.O. Box 9077
Buffalo, NY 14269-9077

In Canada
Gold Eagle Books
P.O. Box 636
Fort Erie, Ontario
L2A 5X3

Please specify book title with your order.
Canadian residents add applicable federal and provincial taxes.

GOUT39

TAKE 'EM FREE
2 action-packed novels plus a mystery bonus
NO RISK
NO OBLIGATION TO BUY

SPECIAL LIMITED-TIME OFFER

Mail to: Gold Eagle Reader Service™

IN U.S.A.:	IN CANADA:
3010 Walden Ave.	P.O. Box 609
P.O. Box 1867	Fort Erie, Ontario
Buffalo, NY 14240-1867	L2A 5X3

YEAH! Rush me 2 FREE Gold Eagle® novels and my FREE mystery bonus. If I don't cancel, I will receive 6 hot-off-the-press novels every other month. Bill me at the low price of just $29.94* for each shipment. That's a savings of over 10% off the combined cover prices and there is NO extra charge for shipping and handling! There is no minimum number of books I must buy. I can always cancel at any time simply by returning a shipment at your cost or by returning any shipping statement marked "cancel." Even if I never buy another book from Gold Eagle, the 2 free books and mystery bonus are mine to keep forever.

166 ADN DZ76
366 ADN DZ77

Name _____ (PLEASE PRINT)

Address _____ Apt. No. _____

City _____ State/Prov. _____ Zip/Postal Code _____

Signature (if under 18, parent or guardian must sign)

Not valid to present Gold Eagle® subscribers.
Want to try two free books from another series? Call 1-800-873-8635.

* Terms and prices subject to change without notice. Sales tax applicable in N.Y. Canadian residents will be charged applicable provincial taxes and GST. This offer is limited to one order per household. All orders subject to approval.

® are trademarks owned and used by the trademark owner and or its licensee.

© 2004 Harlequin Enterprises Ltd.

GE-04R

a priceless artifact sparks a quest to keep untold power from the wrong hands...

Alex Archer
SOLOMON'S JAR

Rumors of the discovery of Solomon's Jar—in which the biblical King Solomon bound the world's demons after using them to build his temple in Jerusalem—are followed with interest by Annja Creed. Her search leads her to a confrontation with a London cult driven by visions of new world order; and a religious zealot fueled by insatiable glory. Across the sands of the Middle East to the jungles of Brazil, Annja embarks on a relentless chase to stop humanity's most unfathomable secrets from reshaping the modern world.

Available September 2006 wherever you buy books.